Edgar Rolfe

1978

MICHAEL POLILLO

Contents

Shoot My Valentine

It was half past three in the morning when Valentine walked through the front door. His wife was sitting in the living room. He didn't know that until she flicked on a light. It caught him off guard and he covered his eyes while they adjusted. They did and the first thing they witnessed was the frown on her face. The second thing he saw were the packed bags at her side and the fact that she wasn't in anything close to a night gown. She had on an open wool jacket and a hat to match.

"I was starting to wonder if you were coming home at all," she said, "I was about to phone the police."

He paced around the living room, unable to make his mind up on sitting or standing.

"It looks like you're about to take off on me. What's this all about? You know I've been working late nights at the mill."

"Yeah and they seem to be keeping you later each week. It was midnight to start. Then after 1. Now it's after 3. Who are you fooling? Cause it isn't me anymore."

"There's no need for concern, Kirsty."

He finally decided to sit down on a short couch across from her. Valentine took off his jacket and placed it beside him. His wife shifted in her seat and buttoned her coat.

"No concern? I can smell her from here. How long has it been going on? Were you ever really working late or was it all bullshit?"

Kirsty Valentine stood and made her way towards the door. She turned around and her husband hadn't budged from the couch.

"You want me to beg you to stay or something? You know I'm not like that. And you know I wouldn't be sleeping around on you," he said.

"I bet you've been saying the same thing to her," she said.

"Come on, it's freezing out there and in the middle of the night. Where are you going to go?"

"I thought you said you weren't going to beg me to stay."

He barely twitched.

"I'm not. You want to go out there? Fine by me. I only want to know where it is you plan to go."

"It's the funniest thing. The office just called me in and wants me to work late."

Valentine turned off the lights and walked out the door.

—

Edgar Rolfe hopped out of his car and headed right towards the Chinese restaurant. A young married couple ran the joint. Sun and Bao Wu; cook and server respectively. Rolfe opened the door with a swift kick. The cook's eyes jumped out of his head and the server beside him started to crack up. He strolled over to one of the stools at the counter. He laid his head down and sprawled out his arms. A customer walked out carrying bags of food without even looking at the man. The rest of the place was empty.

"Long day?" the server asked, "I can tell by the way you're abusing my door. I'm intuitive like that."

Rolfe's eyes looked up without moving his head.

"Don't get me started," said Rolfe.

"Okay, Bao, you heard the man. Don't get him started. We might be able to go a night without him running his mouth for hours," said the cook.

"You like his stories more than I do, Sun," said Bao.

Rolfe had rented from them for five years and talked daily the same. Their arrangement was fine on both ends as long as he made his payments on time. Otherwise he might get a swift talking to or worse, a letter on his door.

He was thirty-five looking forty and stood at a thin five-eight. Few ever saw him not wearing a black suit with a coffee colored collared shirt underneath. It was unknown if he had other clothes or if his entire closet was filled of the same cheap suit like a character in a Hanna Barbera show. No one had the heart to tell him it clashed. That or no one cared. But he knew and he preferred to think no one had the heart.

Bao poured him a glass of water and he downed it graciously. She refilled it and he took it slower this time with sips.

"There's not much of a story today besides being chased by a damn Australian shepherd. I don't even know why they call them that. He sure as hell wasn't carrying a, well I don't know what those hooks are called."

"Crooks," said Sun.

"I don't know how he knows these things," said Bao.

"I would have never guessed it," said Rolfe.

"How did a dog end up chasing you anyway?" said Bao.

"It's simple, really. A woman hired me to go pick up some hidden jewelry she left behind at an old house she sold. I waited all day in my car for the new occupants to leave. Turns out there was a dog left at home," Rolfe downed the rest of his water, "The things I do for a little bit of cash. At least it's better than being shot at."

"How much did you charge for a job like that?" said Sun.

"You being curious, nosey, or worried about me being late on rent again?" said Rolfe.

"All of the above."

Rolfe took out a few bills and slid them across the counter. Sun pocketed them and nodded.

"Let's just say she gave me half of what I asked. She claims the other half will come next week, but we all know how that goes."

"Don't worry about it. We understand," said Bao, "How about some coffee and potstickers? I'm assuming you haven't eaten all day as usual."

"That sounds like a great way to spend the night," said Rolfe, "You really are an intuitive."

Potstickers were his favorite treat to eat after a successful client. Or any client for that matter. Those little crescent moons stuffed with pork and cabbage reminded him of the special pierogies his friend's mother made him when he was a child.

Bao poured him a cup of coffee while Sun started in the back. Rolfe stretched out his arms when another joined them. She had opened the door quietly and tapped her way towards the counter. She was inches away from Rolfe who was doing his best not to look at her. Still she caught his eye. A tall, thin woman with long hair sticking out of a wool hat while wearing a coat to match. He focused his attention back on the coffee.

She spoke with a soft voice, but Rolfe knew those could be deceiving. From ex-wives to countless mistakes, he knew.

"Excuse me, ma'am," she said.

"Hello, how can I help you? Do you want to eat in or take out?" said Bao.

"Neither. I'm looking for the detective who's office is upstairs."

A soft chuckle came from Bao. She cocked her head towards Rolfe who increasingly did his best not to make eye contact. His stool swiveled away from the two women as he drank his coffee.

"Are you Eddie Rolfe?" she said.

Rolfe continued to drink his coffee in silence.

"Please, I need your help."

"Come on Rolfe, talk to her. She seems nice," said Bao.

"I haven't had a bite to eat since last night's dinner. You sure this can't wait?"

"I'd rather it didn't," she said.

"Fine, let's go up to my office. Cancel the potstickers, Sun."

Rolfe finished his coffee in one gulp and he led the way upstairs from outside.

—

"I'm sorry to interrupt your dinner, but why haven't you eaten?" she said.

"You know what it's like to sit in a car with a full stomach while waiting for your mark to appear?"

"Can't say I do."

"It ain't a good feeling. And it's a good thing I was on empty because this dog chased me and I would have emptied myself in my pants if there was anything to drop."

"That's disgusting. Do you talk to all your clients like this?"

"Hey, you're not a client yet. Plus you're the one who asked. Did you think I was fasting? It's not Ramadan yet."

"I don't know what that is."

"Forget it."

He opened his office with a key and they both stepped inside. The lights flicked on revealing a desk, a small television, a couple of chairs, and a couch in a corner. These were the furniture pieces amongst filing cabinets, a coffee pot and drawers.

Rolfe poured himself a cup of cold coffee before sitting behind his desk. He motioned for the woman to sit in front. She did.

"Alright, what's this all about?" he said.

"I want you to kill my husband," she said.

"I'm not a hit man, lady. I could have you arrested for this shit. Are you trying to get me to lose my license?"

"You know I wasn't serious."

"Do I? You'd be surprised at who comes in asking for things."

"So you have been a hit man before?"

"Absolutely not. I barely use my gun and fists. I might be a private eye but I'm not a complete stereotype."

"What's that bottle of whiskey doing here then?"

"A man can't drink after a day's work? Do you want a glass?"

"You going to join me?"

"Maybe if my stomach wasn't on empty. This day old coffee will do for now. Alright Miss Murder let's get down to it. Who told you about me?"

"What are you a secret or something? Maybe I looked up private dicks in the phone book."

"Is that what you did?"

"No as a matter of fact," she paused waiting for him to ask 'what,' but he didn't.

He was slowly sipping his mug and nodded for her to continue.

"A friend of mine told me about you. Greta Wilkins."

Rolfe shifted in his seat. He took out a pad and began jotting down notes.

"I liked Greta. She knew how to use the phone to make an appointment."

"Enough about your stomach. I guarantee I had a worse day than you."

"I didn't mention my stomach that time."

"But you were about to."

"I was only going to say that I helped her find an estranged sister."

"She told me all about it and said I need to go see Eddie Rolfe to help me out."

"Alright I trust that you aren't jerking me along now. I like to know how my clients find me is all. There's nothing secret about it. Word of mouth is the way I keep the lights on and stomach full when I'm not interrupted. So please spread the word about the time I eat dinner and if you found me helpful. And since I'm not willing to kill your husband I must bid you goodnight."

"Before you kick me out, could you at least find out if he's cheating on me or not?"

Rolfe scribbled down more notes. He sipped his coffee and poured the woman some whiskey. He slid it across the desk and she drank it.

"Now that's the stuff that's in my wheelhouse. My rate is fifty bucks a day plus expenses. Are you still interested?"

"I am."

"Alright. What's your name? And what's his name?"

"He's Elliot and I'm Kirsty. Kirsty Valentine."

"Valentine, huh? Seems very thematic for the season."

"What do you mean?"

"What don't you mean? It's Valentine's Day tomorrow isn't it?"

"I can't help that my husband shares his last name with a holiday."

"But you could help not coming to me right before this holiday. You ever get the feeling that someone is writing your life? I do and trust me, the writer isn't good."

A faint smile filled her face. It was a default smile. One she was conditioned to put on while men told jokes that weren't funny and while other women told whispers that weren't nice.

"My maiden named was Lawrence if that makes you feel any better."

He wrote all of this down while taking a deep look at the woman.

"Okay. What makes you think he's cheating on you?"

She drank from the whiskey glass and Rolfe filled it some more.

"He goes out all night, smells of other woman and the other night while he was sleeping I saw a mark on his neck."

"Are you married to Dracula? Because it sounds like you're married to Dracula."

"I bet you make that lame joke with everyone woman who comes in here."

"Nah. Not every woman. Just most."

"You should stop. It's lame and plus it doesn't make any sense. Dracula is the one who does the biting."

"Most people appreciate some levity when dealing with these situations. Your friend Greta cracked up when I suggested her sister was taken by a lake monster."

"I'm starting to regret taking her recommendation and interrupting your dinner."

"I'm only testing the waters here. You're the one who started off with the hilarious suggestion of murder. Do you have any idea who he might be cheating on you with?"

"Someone at work. He's a manager at the grain mill here in Brixton. He's been claiming that they're keeping him there all night, but that stinks to me."

"Sounds like a standard sleeping with the secretary case."

"This might seem boring to you, but this is my life here," she said.

"I'm sorry. Do you have a picture of him that I can see?"

Kirsty Valentine relieved herself of a photo she holding in her purse. Rolfe looked at it. It was their wedding photo. The man matched his wife well. He was tall, dark haired, and thin. They seemed happy. She seemed happy which was a contrast to the faded woman before Rolfe now.

"I guess you're not married to Dracula else this photo wouldn't have turned out. You mind if I keep this?"

"Go ahead, I don't need it."

"Alright Mrs. Valentine. I'll check it out tonight for you. I assume he'll be there again tonight?"

"He should be."

"Great. Do you have somewhere you can stay in the meantime?"

"I'll be going back to Greta's."

She stood and the two shook hands. She gave him a number to call and he added it to his other scribbles. She headed towards the door and Rolfe yelled to her.

"Next time maybe you should marry a man who doesn't have a holiday for a name."

"What do you mean next time?"

"I imagine you don't want to stay with him. Seldom do who step foot in this dungeon."

She walked out without responding. Rolfe poured himself some more old coffee to drink as he gathered his supplies for the night; binoculars, phone whistle, camera, and of course his snub nose revolver.

—

Rolfe decided to skip out on his dinner if it meant spending the night staking out Elliot Valentine. He parked his green '71 Chevy Vega hatchback outside the mill. The gates were wide open and he managed to get in without any notice. The mill had three buildings scattered around its grounds. The biggest was where the real work was done. This is where the detective was planted.

It was already nearing one in the morning. Rolfe had his binoculars on and could easily see Valentine through the wide windows of the mill. Elliot was on the upper floor sitting at a desk writing. This was all he had been doing for the past three hours. The detective snapped a few pictures for evidence and stretched his arms out while yawning.

Maybe the damn woman is nuts. Maybe he really is working late. What do you mean 'maybe?' He clearly is. You've been watching the man fill out paperwork for half the night. Man, I'm starting to get really hungry here. I hope something happens soon.

Rolfe's dreams of potstickers consumed him. *Diced pork, smashed cabbage, that perfect dipping sauce.* He didn't even notice the large man walking towards his car. The man's fist knocked on the detective's window and Rolfe found himself jumping. He turned to his head to see the giant. He had at least a foot on Rolfe and that was telling with the few lights scattered around. They locked eyes with each other while Rolfe cracked the window an inch.

"Could you step out of your car please?" said the giant.

"I'm sorry officer, I'd rather stay inside where it's nice and warm," Rolfe let out a laugh, "I'm just kidding. I know you're not a cop."

The large man didn't return the laughter. He took out a flashlight and shined it around Rolfe's car. He could see the binoculars, camera, and newspaper laying in the passenger's seat. He also saw the slight bulge in Rolfe's jacket that you only know is there if you're looking for it.

"What are you doing out here?"

"Bird watching. You have a problem with a man looking for a pink-footed goose. They're nocturnal, y'know."

"You won't find those around here."

"You're into bird watching too?"

"No. I'm into watching out for little men who snoop around."

"I'll keep a look out for you."

"No thanks, it looks like I found one right here. How about we cut the bullshit and you tell me your name."

"That's all you want to know? I was worried there for a second. I thought you were going to give me a ticket for a broken tail light. My name's Rolfe."

"You mean like the dog?"

"What dog?"

"On the Jimmy Dean show."

"Oh, right. The muppet. You know they got a new show, right? If that helps then yes, but I'm pretty sure it's spelled different."

"I don't give a damn how it's spelled."

"You might if your boss wants to keep tabs on me. I'd hate for that felt dog to take a beating that wasn't for him."

The giant didn't crack the slightest of smiles. It'd be easier to smash a diamond with your hand than getting this beast to chuckle.

"What about you? I'm feeling a little on the line here. You got a name?" said Rolfe.

"You don't need to know my name."

"I guess that makes it easier for when you kill me."

"Take it easy pal. I don't want you here, but that don't make me a murderer."

Rolfe took a closer look at the behemoth at his window. The big man's face looked drained of blood. He was nearly rotting while standing by the car. His nose jutted out a good half foot from his face and it too had a queasy shade of gray to it.

"I'm going to call you Bruno. Bruno the rhino. Normally I'd refer to brutes such as yourself as gorillas or bulls in my inner monologue, but given your nose and complexion, I think a rhino is better suited."

"I don't give a damn what you call me. I need you to leave."

"Why? Are you feeling okay? You want some water or something? I have some coffee here if that'll help."

"What are you talking about?"

"You look like complete shit. You should probably see a doctor about that color consuming your body. That can't be good. I've seen it before, trust me, it never ends well."

The man stuck his fingers in the window and leaned down close, his nose nearly poking through to smell the detective. He was greeted with the distinct scent of coffee mixed with anxiety.

"Let me be clear. Are you going to leave or am I going to have to make you leave?"

"I think you're making me either way. You're in luck, I heard on the radio that there was a booted eagle seen not too far from here. Have a good night, Bruno!"

Rolfe started his car, but the rhino didn't budge.

"One more thing muppet. I'll knock you out if I ever see your face again."

"Oh yeah? That shouldn't be too hard given your two hundred pounds and a foot of height on me."

His eyes squinted down at the detective.

"Or maybe you didn't mean you'd use your fists. You'd get the job done by standing close to me and turning your head quickly. That'd do it."

"I hope I get the chance," said Bruno.

The large man walked away and Rolfe drove his car outside the gates. He turned off his headlights and scratched his head. It wasn't long at all until another set of headlights were coming out of the mill's lot. Rolfe whipped out his binoculars to take a peek. He could tell they belonged to an AMC Hornet. He could also tell that Elliot Valentine was the one driving it.

–

The detective slowly cruised behind the hornet with his lights low and hunger pangs high. It was a quick follow. Valentine went left down a side street then right before slowing down outside a squat house. The house had a neighbor on each side and across the road was all farm. Valentine pulled into the driveway while Rolfe parked on the street at the neighbor's. A light went on and the front door opened. Rolfe had his camera ready. He snapped pictures of a young woman kissing Elliot Valentine at the entrance. She looked familiar. She had that everyday look that has been the thrall of many men. Rolfe had seen it before. *That ain't a kiss you give a friend you hadn't seen in a year. It were a kiss that you give a woman you hadn't seen in five years. And looks like they'd been kissing like this every night with what Mrs. Valentine said. At least it wasn't the secretary at work. The man had no secretary I could see from the hours watching him at his desk.*

Rolfe watched the two of them walk into the living room. He snapped another photo before the woman drew the blinds and he was cut off from any more evidence. His watch told him it was 2:15 a.m. and the only place open to develop pictures was the drive-through. So that's where he went.

It was a small booth in the middle of a parking lot for a short strip mall. It's where Rolfe had gone many nights in order to get his photos done quick and done cheap. He pulled up the window and it opened to a familiar bearded face with a name tag with Kevin written on it.

"They have you on nights again? What happened to the cute girl?" said Rolfe.

"Abby's got the flu. I'm filling in. What's the matter? You don't like to see my beautiful face in the middle of the night?"

"It's not exactly an elixir to keep me going. I'd much rather see the girl. Some nights where it's rough I think about Abby out here manning the booth. And I think, 'if Abby can do it then so can I' and that's what keeps me going."

"Well she's not here. I don't know what to tell you. You're that dick, aren't you?"

"Yeah."

"Anything good tonight?" he paused, "Oh sorry, I bet you can't tell me even if you wanted to."

"You'll find out yourself, won't you? Make sure you keep them safe until I come back. I wouldn't want this evidence falling into the wrong hands."

Rolfe tossed over the film and Kevin nodded.

"How long do you think it'll take?"

"Couple of hours. I've got a few orders to finish before I can get to yours. That okay with you?"

"That's fine by me. I could use some sleep. I was thinking to park my car here and do just that. That okay with you?"

"Fine by me. If any of the Brixton boys bother you, just tell them Kevin's working on your photos."

"Thanks."

Rolfe parked his car and closed his eyes for a minute. The sun was shining faster than he knew it. No cops had bothered him and his watch now told him it was 8:15 a.m. He looked around and no longer found himself in an empty lot. Cars were on all sides of him. Shoppers were carrying balloons, chocolates, and bags of who knows what. *Happy Valentine's Day to me.*

—

Rolfe went through the drive through again, picked up the photos from someone who relieved Kevin and parked again to look through them. They were clearly pictures of Elliot Valentine kissing and sitting with a woman who wasn't his wife. Rolfe went to a payphone in the lot and took out a tiny red whistle from his coat pocket. He lifted the phone, blew into the whistle and dialed the number Kirsty gave him. She answered after two rings.

"Hello, who is it?"

"It's Rolfe, Mrs. Valentine. I've got some bad news for you," he waited for her to ask 'what' and she didn't, "It turns out you were right. Your husband has been seeing another woman. I've got photos of them together proving it. It's a pretty open and shut case if you ask me."

Usually there's sobbing sounds on the other end of these calls, but Kirsty was silent.

"Are you there ma'am?" said Rolfe.

"Yes. Thank you for finding out for me."

"Did you want to meet in person to discuss it more? Do you want the photos?"

"No I don't want the goddamn photos of my husband sleeping with another woman."

"They're not exactly that. Only kissing."

"I don't want to see that either," she said, "Now if you'll excuse me I'd like to be alone with my thoughts."

"What about my payment?"

"I'll get it to you sometime next week."

She hung up and Rolfe put the phone back.

"That's what they all say," he said to no one.

Rolfe reached his office fifteen minutes later. He headed towards the stairs when Bao caught him.

"How'd it go last night?" she said.

"Another case in the books," said Rolfe, "There's no case too tough for this dick."

"That's good to hear. Have you eaten yet?"

"No, I'm only getting home now."

"How about I fix you some breakfast then. What would you like?"

"Is it too early for potstickers?"

"It's never too early for potstickers, Rolfe."

"Alright, let me go freshen my face up a bit and I'll be right back down."

Bao smiled and walked into her restaurant. Rolfe clunked up the stairs and opened his office. The morning light was shining through and he could see large shadow was sitting on his couch. The rhino had come to pay him a visit.

"Hello Bruno," said Rolfe.

"Hello muppet."

"What brings you to my office? Are you worried about Mrs. Bruno going behind your horn?"

"I'm afraid not."

Rolfe flicked on the lights for a better look at the gray man. *At least he's not holding a gun.*

"Don't even think about drawing on me," said the rhino.

Rolfe poured himself a quick cup of two day old coffee and sipped it. The rhino watched his every move without leaving his seat.

"I don't understand what this is all about."

"Mr. Valentine wants me to bring you in so I'm here to bring you in."

Rolfe's stomach gurgled and he put the mug on his desk while pacing around.

"What's a man like that need a hired hand for?"

"Oh you know. The same reasons as anyone. All the heavy lifting can't be down alone."

"That must be horrible for that giant back of yours."

"Don't you worry none, you look pretty light to me, shorty."

The rhino charged the detective with a downward tackle. Rolfe fell to the floor and found himself lifting back up without his consent. Bruno had a hold on shoulders, bringing him face to face.

"You didn't even give me an easy way or the hard way option," said Rolfe.

"I told you, 'I'll knock you out if I ever see your face again,' and I always stand by my promises."

"But you're the one who came here."

"Yeah. Funny how that worked out. Ain't it?"

The rhino's nose curled as he drove a fist into Rolfe's face. The detective fell to the floor once more.

—

Rolfe remembered brief pieces of what happened. He was definitely punched, he still felt that. Then he was tossed into a car and brought somewhere. His mind drifted between worlds. Ultimately it was the sound of his gurgling stomach that returned him to reality. Reality was blurry at first. There were blobs standing around him and floating chunks of fire. *Am I still dreaming?*

The blobs filled out to be people. People he'd seen before and was getting tired of. The rhino was lumbering around in a corner. The Valentines were seated at a table with plates of food and candles to keep them company. Four chairs were seated, but two were empty. Stacked bags of grain were scattered clumsily. *I must be in the mill. Unless they decided to bring me somewhere that looks like a mill to mess with me.*

No one hadn't noticed his return to consciousness. So he took his time to be reacquainted with his body. His nose sniffed the air. Smells of onions, peppers, and steak stuffed his nostrils. That only made his stomach hurt more.

Rolfe wiggled and found himself free. Which was easy given he wasn't tied at all. He saw he was sitting on the floor on a pile of flour. He could feel his gun was gone. He also felt the punch that Bruno had given him to get him here.

Mrs. Valentine was cutting a tiny sliver of steak between bites of onions. It looked like the meat would never be free at the rate she was going. Mr. Valentine was the opposite. He was happily stuffing himself with big chunks using only one hand. The other hand held a gun at his wife across the table. *Wait, what? And that's my gun he's using.*

Rolfe's legs wobbled as he held onto the flour to stand up. The world spun, but only once and he strode over to the table. Rolfe could see that the Valentines didn't see him, but the rhino certainly had. Bruno was charging past the table towards the detective.

"Hey Bruno, take it easy," said Rolfe.

The rhino stopped. The Valentine's turned their heads. Kirsty looked as though the spirit of sadness had possessed her. Elliot was smiling with a smugness seen only on men in his position; holding a gun on their wives while sleeping around on them. Elliot showed the gun to Rolfe to make sure he understood the full picture.

"Please, take a seat," said Elliot.

"You going to join us too, Bruno?" said Rolfe, "I always preferred waiting for the whole family to sit before eating."

Rolfe took a chair in the middle and kept his eyes locked on Mr. Valentine and the gun. The rhino followed suit, sitting across from Rolfe and keeping his hands on the table.

"It's about time we met. Everyone else got to meet you before me. My wife, my hired hand, and finally now it's my turn. I can't say it was worth the wait. You hardly seem worth talking about Mr. Rolfe," said Elliot.

"Thanks. I'm glad you had me knocked out and dragged here to tell me in person. I really appreciate that. It's a nice personal touch."

"I hope he wasn't too rough with you."

"Rough? That guy? I've felt harder punches from a kitten. If that kitten weighed four hundred pounds. Bruno here nearly knocked out one of my teeth with his nose."

"Par for the course isn't it?"

"No. As a matter of fact it isn't. What is wrong with you people? Your wife comes me with the suggestion of killing you then you think I go around getting socked in the face on a regular basis? Do you think I've been itching to shoot someone? Is this God trying to tempt me? Or maybe its Satan. Most of these divorce cases don't end up with one of them dead. Usually I take some pictures and that's the extent of my involvement. I'm not out there as a hired gun."

"You talk a lot for a guy whose mouth is bothering him. Maybe he should hit you again."

The rhino began to stand up from his chair while locking eyes with the detective. His gray fingers were curling into a fist.

"You keep Bruno away from me."

"I don't want to see this," said Kirsty.

She started to stand up away from the table even with the gun still pointed at her.

"Alright, alright, both of you sit back down," said Elliot.

The big man did so without any thought. Kirsty did so slower with as much rebellion as one can while being forced.

"I wasn't going to ask, but I've got to now. Why's he keep calling you Bruno?" said Elliot.

"I don't know. I wouldn't tell him my name so he's been calling me that," said Bruno.

"Hey, I don't mean to interrupt, but do you think maybe you could put the gun down?" said Rolfe.

Mr. Valentine's smile grew even larger. You could see his gums from space.

"I'm sorry, I plan on using it and don't want to lose track of it," said Elliot.

"And what exactly is your plan here? Why did you bother bringing me here? There's got to be something more than just telling me I'm a mediocre detective. I could have called my ex-wife if I wanted to hear that," said Rolfe.

"Show him," said Elliot.

The rhino took out an envelope and laid out the photos on the table. They were of Mr. Valentine and the young woman kissing.

"Kirsty told me that you had photos of me. I wanted to see them for myself. I also wanted to ask you what the fuck do you think you were doing?"

"Yeah I took those, so what? I'm more shocked at you bothering to bring them from my office to here," said Rolfe.

Rolfe grabbed one of the photos and held it close to his face.

"Wait a minute. Is that Abby? I couldn't tell from before, but it definitely is. That little bitch. I can't believe she'd do that to me. And she was supposed to be home sick with the flu!"

"You know her? She's a tempting thing isn't it?" said Elliot.

"She does a great job on my photos. Now I know she photographs well too."

"This isn't meant to be a joke, Mr. Rolfe."

Rolfe tapped on the table while his eyes drooled at the steak.

"You think you could let me get a bite of that before you kill me? I haven't eaten in a while and I'm starving here."

"No, this meal is meant to be my last with my beautiful wife. There's none for you."

"If you've been seeing someone else. Why wouldn't you just divorce your wife?"

"You kidding? She's the one with all the money."

Rolfe shifted his stare to Kirsty Valentine.

"You have money?"

She nodded and broke eye contact.

"Let me guess, she didn't pay you right? This gets better and better. It's the perfect reason. You were angry with not being paid and you decided to get revenge."

"That'll never fly. You know how many people never pay me?"

"It'll have to do."

"You think killing her is going to help your situation?"

"It wasn't my plan, but now I have no choice. She could easily divorce me and leave me not only penniless, but humiliated. But if it's your gun and you have a motive and Bruno here as my witness. I'll inherit her money and you'll inherit all the blame."

Elliot Valentine cocked the gun. Rolfe jumped towards the mill manager. He was too late.

Valentine pulled the trigger, the barrel going off with a loud pop while sending the bullet towards his wife. Her eyes clenched. But she wasn't the one who was hit. Elliot's body fell to the ground on account of Bruno the rhino flipping the table onto him. The bullet went into the ceiling instead of

Kirsty Valentine. Elliot screamed as he was pinned to the ground with Bruno laying on the table.

The hand clutching the revolver was pinched. Rolfe easily grabbed back his gun and holstered it.

The rhino sent a punch into his boss' face and Elliot Valentine went out like a light. Rolfe helped the big man back onto his feet and they both went over to Mrs. Valentine.

"I don't understand. Why'd you do that Bruno?" said Rolfe.

"He didn't say nothing about killing anyone. Especially someone as lovely as Mrs. Valentine here," said Bruno, "I thought I told you earlier that I ain't a murderer."

Kirsty Valentine pummeled her fists into the rhino's chest. He didn't flinch.

"What the hell did you think was going to happen, you absolute idiot?" she said.

The cops came, Elliot was arrested and Rolfe went back to the Chinese restaurant with his fee paid. It was nearly a full twenty four hours since it all started. That meant it had been forty eight hours since the detective ate. He staggered back to the stool at the counter and ordered his potstickers. He ate them quickly as Sun and Bao while asked about his latest case. And then another client walked in.

The Gun With No Brain

It was lightly raining while Rob Bellmore descended the stairs towards his apartment. It was in the basement of a three story complex filled with others like him. Bob was a tall man, at least six-three, but he wasn't built to match his height.

His wife, Whitney was half asleep on the couch with the TV quietly humming.

Rob pulled a blanket over her and sat down with a cold glass of water from the tap. He ran his fingers down her legs and she stirred awake.

"Looks like someone's finally back. I made dinner, but it's more than a little cold now."

"What'd you make?"

"Potato cakes and with black beans."

"That's some combo."

"It's all we had lying around here."

Rob heaved himself from the couch back into the kitchen. There was a plate wrapped in foil on the kitchen table. He opened the fridge and it was empty save for condiments and old milk. He ate the cold meal while standing by the TV.

"How much longer are you going to be coming home at eleven at night?"

"Most wives like it when their husbands work late. Just think of it as me being on a late shift."

"But you're not on a late shift. You're on a second job. One that pays you dirt."

"You know we need the money."

"No shit. That's why I've been picking up extra hours too, but at least I'm home before nine."

"Don't worry, it won't be like this forever."

"Really cause it's been going on a few months and that feels like forever."

"It's going to take some time to pay these debts. I owe money all over Brixton. To the Corbuccis, to the Hillbergs, to the Cygnet gang. I'm probably forgetting someone too."

"Yeah you're forgetting the two men who came here this afternoon," she said.

"What did they look like?"

"They looked mean, Bob."

"What did they say? Who they were?"

"They called themselves the Malloy Boys."

Bob chomped down on a forkful of potato, stuffing it into his mouth and letting pieces fall out as he talked. He scratched his brow before taking another bite.

"That's strange. I don't recall ever borrowing any money from them. I never even heard of them."

"They said they were collectors. They were around your height, but twice as big."

"Collectors? On who's dime?"

"I don't know, but they freaked me out. It's just that these men didn't look like your regular goons. Usually they come by, threaten you or tell me to give you a message, but these two had a different mood. They looked like they wanted to smash my face just for being married to your sorry ass. And they looked like they'd be doing me a favor for doing it too."

"Don't say stuff like that. I wouldn't let them hurt you."

"That's not what I meant. What I meant is that I think they're right. I don't know how much longer I can keep living in debt and watching over our shoulders for strange men who threaten to break kneecaps for late payments."

"Is that what they said? That they're going to break my kneecaps?"

"Isn't that what they always say? You should know by now."

"Maybe we should skip town. You ever think about it?"

Whitney tossed the blanket off and grabbed a coat. She slipped it on along with her purse and headed for the door. Rob put down his plate and put himself between his wife and the exit.

"Where are you going? I was only joking about skipping town."

"Out."

"You were just sleeping."

"That makes me well rested for a night out on the town."

"Are you going to that bar again? You know how I feel about that place."

"I'll go wherever I want."

"It's not. It's that we can't afford it. You think I don't want a drink sometimes? I'd love one."

"I'm sure there'll be someone there who'll buy me one."

"Fine, you think I care? Go ahead."

Rob opened the door and moved aside. Whitney shut the door behind her and began her climb up the stairs towards the rainy street.

—

It was 1 a.m. in the office of Edgar Rolfe. He was sitting at his desk watching his twelve inch black and white TV. The Last Man on Earth was playing while hosted by Brixton's own horror host, Halloween Jack. Rolfe watched Vincent Price running towards a funeral pyre while cleaning his .38 detective special. It laid disassembled on his desk while he ran a bore brush through the barrel. He sipped a small glass of straight whiskey as he dipped the brush into the cleaning solvent.

There's no better way to spend a Saturday than watching horror and a little gun maintenance.

Halloween Jack was parading onscreen. He was wearing an orange suit with a green tie. That was his standard outfit while discussing films no one else cared about. Of course only those with color TVs knew that. And Rolfe only knew that from seeing him once or twice around downtown Brixton. The detective never did get the nerve up to talk to him despite watching his show every week he could.

He smiled and took another sip. That's when he heard a knock at his door. *That's just the wind isn't it? Damn rain is getting worse out there.*

He continued to clean his gun when another fist hit. *Alright, that's not the storm.*

Who the hell is bothering me this late? I'm up to date on my rent, aren't I? Not that the Wus ever come up here this late. Whoever it is, maybe they'll go away if I don't answer. I need to be really quiet.

Rolfe turned off the TV and his desk lamp. He sat in the dark while counting the seconds.

This bastard better go away before this commercial break ends. I want to see what happens to Vincent Price.

Another knock came at the door. Then another. *Fine. I better check it out before they smash the window. At least they can smash my face instead and there'll be less of a mess that way.* Rolfe flicked back on the light and made his way over to his door.

"Hold on, I'm coming. I'm coming."

Maybe it's a beautiful woman come to take all my problems away. Yeah and maybe she's a million bucks with a magic wand that can conjure infinite cupcakes.

The detective peaked through the blinds and saw a tall man standing outside in the rain. It's never good to see a man standing outside your door after midnight. Especially when that man easily has half a foot of height on you. Rolfe did the only thing he could do. He pointed down to the sign on the door that read *closed.*

"We're closed. Come back tomorrow."

A frown came over the tall man's face.

"Please. It's important. I wouldn't be here if it wasn't."

"Don't you see my office hours?"

"There's nothing listed on the door."

"That doesn't matter. What would make you think that a private detective is in his office at 1 in the morning? Shouldn't you know any business isn't open this late?"

"I saw that the light was on."

"Okay but that doesn't answer my question."

"Someone told me that you live here. Is that true?"

"Who told you that?"

"I'd rather not say. I don't think you'd care much for the source considering she clearly didn't care much for you."

And he didn't have to finish for Rolfe to know.

"Fine. But tell her I don't give a damn who knows that I live in my office," he tapped on his door with the gun bore, "Actually don't tell her anything. I don't want her thinking I knew who she was without you telling me."

"I won't. But you're up now, aren't you?"

"Yes, I'm up. You're not talking to someone who's sleepwalking."

"Then could I please come in?"

"Okay, but this better not be a damn lost puppy routine."

Rolfe opened the door. The tall man extended his hand.

"I'm Rob Bellmore."

"Get inside Rob Bellmore."

Rolfe flicked on the lights in his office. The pull out couch in the corner had blankets and pillows ready for a night's rest. Rob glanced at it as he followed the detective to his desk and took the seat in front. Pieces of revolver were still scattered around on top with a half drank glass of whiskey.

"Drinking and cleaning your gun?"

"Yeah and watching Halloween Jack."

"Sounds like a busy night."

"I'd rather be doing that than whatever bullshit you're about to tell me."

"It's not bullshit. I need your help."

Rolfe filled his glass back up and poured another for his potential client. Rob eagerly grabbed the glass and drank.

"Been a while, has it?"

"You don't even know. I've had to make a lot of cutbacks. Drinking was the first."

"That's a shame to hear," Rolfe glanced Bellmore over, "You know, a man of your size looks like he should be able to handle himself on his own. What do you need my help for?"

"You'd think so. It ain't all it's cracked up to be. Everyone wants to start a fight with the tall guy. I can't find peace anywhere."

"Don't give me that wandering samurai crap. We all have our problems in life. It ain't easy for any of us."

"You know how it is. It's the same shit all over. Thugs are everywhere. You couldn't escape them if we were back in Vietnam."

"I wouldn't know."

"You didn't go to 'Nam? I thought all you types were in the service."

"I wasn't picked and sure as hell wasn't going to volunteer."

Rob took a long sip of the whiskey. Rolfe followed suite.

"Yeah well you're better off. I would have gone to Canada if I could."

"That's what I hear. What I don't hear is what the hell you're here for."

"What do you mean?"

"You've been here a few minutes and haven't told me a damn thing. All I know is that you're broke and that you're drinking my whiskey while I should be the only one drinking whiskey and watching old movies."

"It's my wife. She's gone."

"Now we're getting somewhere."

Rolfe took out his note pad and began writing.

"What happened? Was she kidnapped? Was she taken into the sky by invaders from another planet? What's her name?"

"No, she took off on me. Her name is Whitney."

"What does she look like?"

Rob handed over a photo. She had black hair chopped to her shoulders and a smile that hung above a well endowed chest.

"When did it happen? Yesterday? Last week?"

"A few hours ago."

"That explains why you're here now. You couldn't stomach sleeping knowing she's out there and not knowing where. And now you need help tracking her down? Any idea where she may be?"

"Oh I know exactly where she is. She's at a bar."

Rolfe stopped writing and squinted at the man. He turned on the TV and saw Vincent Price running around. Rob Bellmore glanced at the TV behind him and returned sitting forward.

"What are you doing?"

"I'm watching my movie."

"Why?"

"Because your wife is at a bar. You know what bar she's at. You're wasting my time. Go get her yourself."

"I can't get her myself because she won't come home with me."

"But you think she'd come home with me?"

He nodded. Rolfe turned off the TV once more. He picked up his pencil and resumed writing.

"Alright, I won't hold any judgment. What's the place?"

"You know that old bar at the edge of town?"

"Jack's or Bennie's?"

"Jack's."

"Yeah, I know it."

"That's usually where she goes to clear her head."

"So you expect me to take this job when you just told me you don't have any money?"

"I was told you let people pay later."

"And who told you that?" Rolfe paused, "Wait a minute, same source as earlier, am I right?"

Rob nodded. Rolfe put on his coat and headed towards the door, guiding Rob along with him.

"Was that your car out there?" said Rob.

"Which one?"

"The ugly green piece of shit Vega hatchback."

"Yeah, why is it on fire?"

"No, I'm just wondering why a dick would drive a car that brings attention to himself?"

"You want to buy me a new one?"

Rolfe took down Bellmore's number and address.

"Don't worry, I'll get her back to you. We'll continue our discussion of payment later."

Rolfe climbed into his car and headed to the edge of town. *I knew I shouldn't have answered the damn door. It's never a beautiful woman this late at night.*

—

Jack's bar was located on the east edge of Brixton. It was set in a lower income neighborhood and had been there as long as Rolfe can remember. He had driven by it many times without stepping foot inside. It had a brick front that showed its age. A few cars were parked on the street, but Rolfe got lucky. He found a nice spot around the corner for his Vega and headed in. A bouncer stood at the door barring him from going any further. The strong man looked the detective over from head to toe. From his black jacket to tan shirt and tan tipped shoes.

"You know where you're at, right?" said the bouncer.

Rolfe took a step back and pointed to the neon sign above that read Jack's with the 'a' and 's' unlit.

"Looks like I'm at Jack's," said Rolfe.

"Yeah, alright, you don't need to get smart with me. I'm only trying to make sure there's no trouble tonight. You're not going to be any trouble are you?"

"I'm hardly any trouble. I don't plan on staying long anyway.

"Now that sounds like trouble. You're not a cop, are you?"

"No, I'm a private investigator."

"Like Dick Tracy?"

"Dick Tracy isn't a private eye."

"Who fucking cares? I'm throwing your ass out if you so much as drop a glass in there, Tracy," he said.

"You saying I can go in?"

"Yeah and don't make me regret it."

Rolfe walked in and could feel the eyes on him. It wasn't crowded which only led to the feeling that everyone inside was checking out the detective. It was a dimly lit place with a live band in the corner playing some light jazz. Green tablecloth covered tables were placed about with a bar on a far wall. Rolfe couldn't see his mark in the faces that clearly marked him.

A young woman with tied back hair was operating the bar. Rolfe ordered a beer and she brought it over within a minute. The others at the bar backed away as Rolfe drank.

They continued to look at him like a leper. The bartender resumed her duty of keeping the top clean.

"Why's everyone giving me the death glare?" said Rolfe.

She stopped wiping down the counter and addressed the detective directly.

"Take a look at yourself, how you're dressed, how you're walking. I'd say your complexion isn't doing you any favors either. People might get the wrong idea seeing you in here. They might start thinking we're allowing in cops."

"Yeah like I told the doorman, I'm not a cop. I'm a private detective."

"In some ways that's worse, isn't it? Who holds you accountable?"

"Myself."

"That tells me everything right there."

Rolfe looked around at the faces who wouldn't take their eyes off him, but also wouldn't get too close.

"Listen, I'm not here to cause any arguments or arrest anyone or anything like that."

"Then what are you doing in here?"

"I'm looking for a Whitney Bellmore. You know her?"

Rolfe took out a picture and showed it to the bartender. He watched as her eyes scanned every detail before handing it back.

"I don't know the name, but I've seen that face tonight."

"You mind pointing out her direction?"

"If it means getting you out of her sooner? Definitely."

The bartender gestured towards a table that was near the jazz band. There were three people sitting there. Two women and one man. And she was one of the women. Rolfe could tell from the side profile. She stuck out like a sore thumb once pointed out. The detective left a handsome tip, pocketed the photo and grabbed his beer. He slowly walked over and took a seat.

The three set of eyes looked at him with contempt. Rolfe put his beer down before raising his hands.

"Hey, let's cool with the hateful eyes for a second."

"What are you doing around here pig? I don't see any mud here for you to play in," said the man.

"I'm not a cop."

"Then why you dressed like one?" said the other woman.

"Why does everyone think I'm a cop tonight? Have any of you ever even seen a cop before? I'm not a cop. I'm a private detective and my name's Rolfe."

"That's the same shit to me," said the man.

"Now that I think of it, I don't think I'd ever see a cop in colors that clash that much," said Whitney.

"Alright dick, what are you doing here?" said the woman.

Rolfe downed half the beer and pointed to Whitney with his glass.

"Your man wants you to come home," said Rolfe.

Whitney's eyes widened. Her chest heaved and her cheeks puffed out.

"I can't believe he sent someone after me," she said.

"I can't believe it either. I was having a nice night in before your husband came a knocking. Now I'll never know how the Last Man on Earth ends."

"He gets killed," said the woman.

"Thanks," said Rolfe, "Now are you going to make this easy or are you going to make a scene?"

"Why shouldn't I make a scene? I don't want to go back home right now. I don't know if I'll ever want to go back."

Whitney's eyes were filling with tears. Her sobs were vocalizing and she was heaving more. Rolfe's fingers curled on his glass. If the eyes were on him before then the fists were nearly on him now. He could see at least three men nearly raising out of their chairs.

"You heard her man, she don't want to go with you. So why don't you get out of here before we throw you out?" said the man.

"Come on lady. Everyone in this place is already looking for a reason to knock me out. I don't want to do this anymore than you do."

Whitney wiped her tears with her sleeve and drank from her own glass. The other faces around them returned to their own company.

"Alright, I'll go with you, but I'm not going home," she said.

"Okay. If that's a start to get us out of here then I'll take it."

Rolfe left his chair and waved goodbye to the others sitting at the table. Whitney followed him out the front door and they stood by the bouncer.

"Yes, I'm sure," said Whitney.

"Alright. I didn't hear any trouble in there. You kept your word, Tracy. I'm surprised."

"I'm a little surprised myself. I thought I was going to get knocked out."

"Take care, little man," said the bouncer.

They started down the street towards Rolfe's car around the corner.

"Why'd he call you Tracy?" said Whitney.

"He's got a crush on me," said Rolfe.

She let out a laugh from the belly all the way up. And it was nice to see. What wasn't nice to see were the two big men walking their way. They looked nearly identical to each other. They wore dark blue suits with no ties and no hats on their bald heads. Whitney grabbed for Rolfe's arm and Rolfe grabbed for his .38 special, but found his holster empty. *Shit, I forgot to take my gun. Shit! I forgot to even reassemble my damn gun.*

"Give us the girl and be on your way," said one of the them.

"I don't think that's going to happen."

"This doesn't concern you, shamus," said the other.

"It does if you're trying to steal my client."

Rolfe planted his feet and slipped on his tan gloves, the cookers. He swung one cooker at the closest thug and landed perfectly on the bald face. The other thug grabbed Rolfe and sent three quick jabs into the detective's side. Rolfe struggled to stand. He fell when the first thug returned and kicked out Rolfe's legs. One picked him up and the other sent a punch into the detective's face. A slight click was heard and a woman shouted.

"Get the fuck away from him," said Whitney.

Rolfe looked up to see the woman holding a small strange looking pistol at one of the thug's heads.

"You know how to use that thing?" said the thug.

"I think anyone could at this range," she said.

They dropped the dick and backed off.

"You'll be seeing us again soon, Mrs. Bellmore."

The two men took off down the street. Whitney helped stabilized Rolfe until he found himself able to breathe on his own again.

"Who were they?" said Rolfe.

"The Malloy boys. Collectors for my husband's debt. They came to my apartment this afternoon, but I don't know why they'd come after me."

"Looks like they want you to be collateral."

Whitney helped Rolfe towards his car and they both climbed inside.

"You want me to drive instead?"

"I'll be alright. Just give me a minute."

"Alright."

"I didn't think this was going to be one of those nights. Just what exactly is your husband wrapped up in?"

"He's in a lot of debt. He owes money to any and everyone in Brixton who'd give him any."

"What the hell for? Is this a tearjerker? His mom dying and he needs the money to save her? You got a kid who's only got one leg and two fingers?"

"No. He likes to gamble."

"That was going to be my third guess."

"What's that weird gun you're carrying?"

Whitney took out the pistol and let Rolfe examine it. It had white grips and nickle plating with *Whitney* engraved on it. He opened the magazine to see ten .22 rounds inside. *Not much of a gun.*

"Looks like something out of that Star Wars move."

"He got it for me because my name's on it. You believe that? Someone decided to name their gun, Whitney."

"Hey it doesn't get easy to give gifts as the years go on."

"Where's your gun anyway? Don't tell me you're one of those pacifist types."

"No, I have a gun. Your husband interrupted me while I was cleaning it and I didn't manage to put it back together before coming to pick you up."

"Why don't you take mine then? I'm a terrible shot."

"I don't think that'll be necessary."

"You never know. I want you to hold onto it until this is over."

Rolfe looked over the woman and she nodded. He slipped the gun into his inside pocket.

"Are you married, Mr. Rolfe? I don't see a ring on your finger."

Rolfe stirred in the driver's seat.

"Why don't you ask your husband? He seems buddy enough with my ex to know I live in my office."

"Must be one of his friends. He's never mentioned knowing any woman who was with a detective before, Mr. Rolfe. So you have been married then?"

"Rolfe's fine. Lose the Mister. And yes, I've been married twice."

"You mind me asking what happened?"

"I'm guessing there's no way out of it now. The first one left me for another man. Second one left me for another life."

"You mean she died? That makes so much sense."

"What does?"

"That's why you're a private dick now, right? You're trying to find out who killed your wife while helping others?"

"No, I know who killed her."

"Oh."

"How about we get going? You hungry?"

—

Rolfe started the car and headed back to his office. She took a seat on the couch while he got her something to drink that wasn't alcohol. He brought over a bag of pretzels and handed them to her. Whitney turned on the TV and there was only static.

"You like Halloween Jack too?" she said.

"How did you know that?" said Rolfe.

"You mentioned that you were watching the Last Man on Earth. That's what he was showing tonight. I decided to go to the bar instead."

"Yeah I try to watch him every week if I'm not out picking up stray wives."

"Maybe next week we can watch it together."

"Only if your husband is there with us."

She turned the TV off and didn't touch the water he had given her. She picked up a pretzel and crunched down on it hard.

"You're all business aren't you, Mr. Rolfe? We'd gladly have you over."

"It's the least you can do considering your husband has no money."

She nodded and finally took a sip of the water.

"You think maybe we should get back to him? He's bound to be worried."

"I thought you'd let me stay here."

"Only until your head cleared. This is hardly a place for anyone to stay."

"Isn't there anything you can do to help? Is it even safe to bring me back there?"

"Do you want to get the police involved?"

"God, no, that'd only make everyone more mad."

"Then there's not much I can do. I can't take on every loan shark and gangster in Brixton. I'm not a vigilante, Whitney. I'm one man trying to get by."

"I know," she paused to give a long sigh, "Alright, take me home."

They headed outside and Rolfe barely felt the butt of the shotgun smashing into his skull. He looked up to see the Malloy Boys carrying a wiggling Whitney into a black sedan. Her mouth was covered so her eyes did the screaming for her. Rolfe staggered to his feet and threw up once. One of his teeth was feeling more loose than usual. He prodded it with his tongue while he made his way to his Vega.

—

Rolfe parked his car in front of the apartment building. He fell down the last two steps before knocking on the door.

Bob Bellmore opened the door and he wasn't looking much better. His left eye was swollen and his right arm seemed more limp. Rolfe pushed his way in and sat on the couch. The room revealed itself to him. Broken plates, chairs, and the kitchen table were smashed. The TV however was untouched and filled with static. The two men didn't say anything for the first minute. Bellmore brought the detective something for his head and Rolfe gagged while trying to down some gin. A small piece of tooth came up with it. He tossed it aside before addressing his kind host.

"They took her," said Rolfe.

"Yeah I didn't think she was the one to clock your head."

"What exactly did you drag me into here? All I wanted to do was watch shitty movies and you had to bring me into the crosshairs of loan sharks."

Bellmore filled his glass of gin up and chugged it before filling it again. He rubbed at his limp arm and his lips trembled.

"They came here and wanted money. I didn't have any. Then they said I'd regret that. I didn't think they'd take her."

"Of course you did. That's why you wanted me to go find her in the first place."

"I thought a guy like you would keep her safe," he drank more, "I don't understand it. Why didn't she use her gun?"

"I have it. Someone interrupted me during my cleaning and I forgot to grab my own gun."

Rolfe took the gun out from his pocket. He held it up as if that'd help somehow.

"I need you to get out there and find her."

"Sure, let me just call up my friend the tooth fairy and she'll tell me where two goons took your wife. Or maybe we'll wait for her to call and she'll even give us a piece of candy for being such good boys."

"Isn't this the type of shit you do?"

"Absolutely. But typically I look for any witnesses who last saw the missing person. Guess who that was?"

The phone on the wall rang. Bellmore got up and stood idle by it. Rolfe gestured for him to answer. It was them.

"Where is she? What have you done with her? You better not have hurt her," said Bob.

Rolfe perked his ears to listen to no avail. He watched Bellmore's reactions to make up for it.

"When?" he paused, "At the lake?" he drank more gin, "Yes, I'll be there."

Bellmore hung up the phone and finished the bottle.

"Let me guess, the standard? They want the money and you'll see your wife in good health only when they get it? And they want it delivered at the lake in an hour?"

"So this is the type of shit you do. They want us at the lake within an hour with a hundred thousand dollars. What's the plan here?"

"I think now's a good time to get the police involved."

"That isn't an option. They'd only have me arrested."

"Not necessarily."

"No. There's got to be another way."

"You know anyone that can lend you the money?"

"No. I've already borrowed from the Corbuccis to pay back the Cygnets. And I still owe both of them payments. I don't even know who these guys are."

All I know about these guys are that your wife called them the Malloy Boys. I've never heard of them. Trust me, I know all the different pieces of shit that come through this town."

"I already knew their name, but that doesn't help much."

"You have no money, but do you have any other guns?"

"You kidding? I had sell all of them to help pay back these assholes. Whit only kept hers because they didn't know about it."

Rolfe managed to finish his glass of gin.

"Well we better go anyway. Maybe they'll cut you a deal."

"What sort of a deal?"

"One that'll be hard to walk away from."

—

Rolfe dropped Bellmore off at the lake before parking his car out of view. He was on his own now and hopefully wouldn't ruin it before the detective got into place. Rob Bellmore could see the Malloy Boys standing with his wife nearby. The boys were mountainous with slicked back hair wearing gray jackets. One had a shotgun in his hands and the other held a pistol. The lake was calmly crashing on the sand with the morning sun showing itself over the water. Bellmore approached them with caution, holding his hands in the air and making sure his movements were slow.

"You alone?" said the shotgun.

"You said to be alone, didn't you?" said Bellmore.

"We're making sure you can follow directions," said the pistol.

"Looks like we scared that shamus off. I knew a little man like that was a pussy," said the shotgun.

"Not like Bellmore here's much better. He hired that little man to protect his wife," said the pistol.

"We shouldn't be complaining. It makes our job easier," said the shotgun.

Bellmore was closer to them and could see the sadness in Whitney's eyes. She wasn't gagged, but she clearly had been told to keep quiet.

"Who are you bastards anyway?" said Bellmore, "I don't remember taking any money from you."

"Didn't your wife tell you? We're collectors. We've come to collect," said the pistol.

"Yeah, but for who?"

"For all of them. How long did you think you could keep getting away with borrowing money to pay others? Someone worked out your little scheme and we're here for all the money," said the shotgun.

"You didn't say all the money on the phone. You only said a hundred thousand."

"Don't wet yourself Bellmore. We're not monsters. You'll be giving it to us in ten installments," said the shotgun.

"Speaking of, where's the money?" said the pistol.

Rob reached into his pocket and pulled out a stuffed envelope. The pistol brother grabbed it and immediately tore it open. Pieces of wood, newspaper clippings, and other shrapnel from their attack on the apartment spilled onto the ground. The pistol cocked and Whitney let out a yelp.

"Do you think this is some sort of joke?" said the shotgun.

"What did you expect? Every last mobster in Brixton knows I'm broke."

"We thought you'd at least have the dignity to die without pulling this shit."

Whitney ran over to Rob and clung to him.

"Out of the way bitch, your husband doesn't respect anyone and we're not letting him steal any more money," said the shotgun.

"Go ahead and kill me, but let her go for the love of God."

"Sure, we'll let her go right after she sees what happens to low lifes like you. Try anything and he'll blow her head off with the shotgun before I put one in you."

The pistol brother aimed the gun at Bellmore's chest. A pop went off and a scream followed. A louder blast followed that and second small pop was the last shot fired. Three men collapsed to the ground. One man stepped forward out from a bush. Rofle had hit the shotgun Malloy with his Whitney. That brother sent buckshot into his other brother's head. And that poor Malloy's last action on Earth was to squeeze his trigger, sending a bullet into Rob Bellmore's left knee.

Whitney knelt by her husband, cradling him in her arms. Rolfe took a look at the mangled head that was once a man. It was hard to make out any facial features in the mix of blood and bone. He could hear scuffling and turned to see the shotgun Malloy trying to get back up. Rolfe grabbed the shotgun and told him to stay down or he'd be joining his brother. The Malloy clutched at his chest, trying to find where Rolfe had hit him.

"Don't worry, you'll live and get to spend plenty of time in jail thinking about how you killed your brother."

The Malloy opend his mouth, but Rolfe silenced him with the shotgun barrel in his face.

"Save it for the cops," said Rolfe.

Lights could already be spotted coming down the road. The sirens were blasting and three patrol cars soon pulled up. An ambulance came a minute later.

"I thought I said no cops," said Bellmore laying on the ground, "When did you even have the time to call them?"

"There's a phone at the maintenance building. What did you think took me so long?"

"I thought you took off on us," said Whitney.

"I can't abandon a client. Especially one that I know doesn't have the money to pay me anything."

"Consider keeping that gun as a down payment."

The cops took their statements, took away the living Malloy, and told Rob that'd he'd make it. They helped him into the ambulance and Whitney climbed in, waving goodbye to the detective.

—

"On tonight's show, I'll be guiding you through a world of ghouls and ghosts in another Vincent Price feature, The House on Haunted Hill."

Rolfe's eyes were glued to the TV. He could truly see all the detail and color in Halloween Jack's costume on the full 16 inches of screen. The movie started in black and white and that's when he finally moved back to the couch. Whitney and Bob were already there and the detective squeezed in on the end. Bob Bellmore had his leg up and Whitney had her arm down in a bowl of popcorn.

"How many more Saturday nights are you going to spend here, Rolfe?" said Rob.

"Oh come on honey, without him you'd either be dead or in jail," said Whitney, "At least those other sharks are scared to death now of the man who took out one of the Malloy boys."

"Better they think it was you than me," said Rolfe.

Rolfe stuffed a handful of popcorn in his mouth and turned his attention back to the movie.

Shelter Skelter

Fog flooded the air of the warm June night in Brixton. All that could be seen was a humanoid figure making his way down the streets in the east side of town. He was wearing three layers of loose clothing despite the heat that comes with summer in New Jersey. His mind barely noticed. Just as it barely noticed the bulky bag he dragged at his side down the sidewalk. The streetlights were the only beacons guiding his way. Except he had no way. There was no destination in mind for this man. He had gone to the Brixton shelter a few hours earlier and he was too late. They were filled to capacity leaving him to roam the streets until morning when he could return for stale muffins and warm milk. And so he did as many do when it the nights are young, he wandered. Other figures slipped in and out of the fog, moving silently without purpose, without hope as they killed time. Some clutched half drank bottles of gin, others dug through bins, but the trash in east Brixton had little in it. It was considered a good night when you found pizza crust. It was a great night when you found stray fries in a bag.

Our man hit the jackpot earlier in the night. Someone had thrown a bag out with a half eaten burger and two fries still inside. He stuffed that unwanted bag into the duffel he was lugging and kept walking. The man's eyes strained at a new source of light was speeding down the road. It was unusual for cars to be out this late on this side of town. The lights darted all over the street. The man picked up his pace, trying to avoid what was barreling down the row in his direction.

He ran faster, dragging his duffel behind before dropping it entirely. His legs lifted as high and spread as they could as the lights gained closer. He could only see fog mixed with shadows from the car behind him. The sounds of the engine took over his pounding heart and stampeding footsteps. He flew through the air with a brick wall breaking his fall. He had screamed and no one had listened. The beams stopped, hovering in mid-air, the engine growing quiet. He looked up to see a set of legs standing before him. They took a half step before the lights took them back. And then the lights were gone.

The man laid in silence, letting his last moments on Earth be still. He closed his eyes and he too was gone.

—

Edgar Rolfe pushed open the door to the Chinese restaurant. He was greeted with an egg roll sent flying towards his face. His hands caught it with ease and he chomped down on it before taking a stool by the front the counter. The man who tossed it, Sun Wu, was now stirring a wok in the kitchen. Wu barely acted as if he had seen the detective come in, despite throwing him a treat.

"This a new recipe?" said Rolfe.

The cook smiled.

"Nope, you must have new taste buds."

"Hey, I didn't say it was bad or anything, but you went a little heavy on the cabbage."

"You better watch what you say, I didn't make that batch. Bao's been working on her cooking."

"If Bao made these then it's the best egg roll I've ever had. Just what I needed after a long morning of waiting for a man with a broken leg to go dancing."

"Did he?"

"All the way to the bank to cash his insurance check."

He stuffed the rest of the egg roll into his mouth and chugged a glass of water.

The front door opened and a familiar face was there. Bao Wu, wife and main hostess was carrying in a large box. Rolfe hurriedly went to her aide, taking the box away and dropping it in the kitchen.

A visible bump could be seen around her belly. And while Rolfe knew never to ask a woman if she's expecting, this was different. He had known of the good news for some time. And unfortunately knew they were trying for even longer.

"Thanks uncle Rolfe," she said.

Bao Wu sat down behind the counter and smiled.

"I thought I said stop it with the 'uncle Rolfe' stuff."

"What would you rather us call you around the baby?"

"Just Rolfe is fine."

"You're family to us, you're going to be family to the baby too," said Sun.

"Family who happens to pay for the office above your restaurant."

"Yes, exactly. Family who we barely bug when he's behind on rent and who we tend to feed for free on top of it," said Bao.

Rolfe stirred in his seat as Sun brought him a plate of vegetable lo mein and fried rice.

Sun and Bao hugged each other and Sun's hand gently touched his wife's belly.

"Any kicking yet?"

"Not yet, it's still a little early, but any day now we'll be wishing it never started," she said.

"I can't wait," said Sun.

"I've told her to hurry up because uncle Rolfe here is waiting," said Bao.

Rolfe stuffed a forkful of lo mein into his mouth. Then the door opened again. It wasn't a familiar face this time. A middle aged woman was standing with a confused look on her face. Her hair was strung out as if she hadn't slept in a few days and her eyes could carry an elephant in them. Rolfe scooped up some rice as he watched it. *Who am I to judge who comes in for some food? She probably needs a nice warm meal. She's fine as long as she ain't bothering me. I've got my food, a day's pay, and the rest of the afternoon to nap away.*

The woman made her way to the counter and was met with the smiling Bao.

"Can I help you?"

"I'm looking for Edgar Rolfe. When's he usually in?"

Bao pointed to the man who was within a foot of them. Rolfe turned with a huff.

"Yeah, yeah I'm right here. Can't you see I'm trying to eat? My office sign said, 'out to lunch,' and that's what I'm trying to do here. So if you don't mind, I'll be in my office in an hour."

He chomped down on some fried rice and turned away from her.

The frazzled woman spoke with a kindness in her voice.

"I'm sorry to bother you, but it's important."

Rolfe slurped down more noodles. *It's always important, isn't it? Just once I'd like them to say, 'okay, I'll come back later.' Yeah, like that would ever happen.*

The detective faced the woman and talked with his mouth full.

"Alright, fine. Usually I don't talk business outside the office, but I'm starving. So what's the scuttlebutt?"

"Scuttlebutt?"

"Yeah, you think your husband is cheating on you? You lost a dog and want me to find him? You in over your head in a money laundering scheme?"

"No, nothing like it."

Rolfe shoved more food into his stomach.

"How about you tell me then? Or do you want to me pull it out of you?"

"It's about a murder."

Rowlf dropped his fork.

"Not another word," he said, "Head upstairs."

The woman followed his directions and left the restaurant.

Rolfe stood up off the stool and looked at the Wus who were trying not to laugh. Not that murder is a laughing matter, but that the detective was interrupted yet again.

"History repeats itself, doesn't it?" said Sun.

"Not this time," said Rolfe.

He carried the plate out of the restaurant and headed to his office. He quickly unlocked it and the two went inside.

He motioned for her to sit and he didn't offer her a drink.

Rolfe had been close enough to the woman to pick up on the scent of alcohol that clung to her and her clothes. He wasn't against a drink or two, but she smelled more like a case of whiskey over a bottle. *Might be a good idea not to feed her any more.* He placed his plate down on his desk and took smaller bites as he talked.

"Alright ma'am, how about we start over?"

"I don't know where to begin," she said.

"Your name would be a good place."

She shifted in the chair and her eyes were darting around the room.

"My name is Ida Keyes."

"See? That's not a bad beginning. I do need a little bit more though. Like what's this talk of murder and how can I factor into it?"

Her eyes focused back on the detective and the meal he was eating.

"Maybe a drink would help," she said.

"Maybe you've had enough already."

"I'm sorry if I seem drunk. This day has been a blur. I can barely remember getting the call this morning."

"What call is that?"

"The one saying my brother had been killed in a hit and run."

Rolfe pushed his plate to the side and grabbed his notepad. He began scribbling as she went on. Rolfe poured her a small glass of whiskey and handed it to her. She drank it in one gulp and he filled it again.

"They don't know who did it."

"And you want me to find out? A hit and run doesn't mean a murder. Accidents do happen."

She sipped at her second glass.

"I think someone wanted him dead."

"I'm not sure this is my type of case. This is something that the cops should handle if there's a bigger motive."

"They already decided it wasn't worth their time."

"Why not? Hit and run cases still need to be solved even if they aren't a planned murder."

She drank the rest of her glass down.

"Because he was homeless. 'Who gives a fuck about a dead bum?' they said. Even after what I told them, they weren't interested."

Rolfe scribbled down more notes.

"So, not to be rude, but why do you give a fuck about a dead bum?"

"Wouldn't you want to know who killed your brother? He may have been a bum, but he was still family."

"I don't have a brother."

"I'm sure there's someone else you'd care about then. We've all got families."

He slurped up more noodles and drank some whiskey himself.

"What makes you think I can find the person who killed your brother if the cops aren't even bothering to?"

"Because like I told them, I have an idea who did it."

Rolfe finished his plate and put his full attention on the woman.

"Y'see, he was an artist. A damn good one too, but no one else thought so. That's why he ended up on the streets."

"What are you trying to say? You think someone killed him for his art? An old rival maybe?"

"I think it's more than that. Have you heard of the Wool gallery?"

"No, is it full of knit art? Bunch of scarves, mittens, and hats?"

She stared at the detective, stifling a scream.

"Wool is the name of the owner. He specializes in local art. All the best in the tri-state area are shown there. Rich folk come from all over to add pieces to their collections."

"And you think this Wool killed your brother? Why? What would he have to gain from that?"

"He'd gain notoriety for having a collection of art from a dead artist. He'll probably want to buy what I have of my brother's paintings off me within a week."

"Why would anyone care if he's dead if they didn't buy his stuff when he was alive?"

"You know nothing about the art world, do you?"

She glanced around his office at the off color walls, mismatching furniture and the suit he was wearing. Black and tan mixed together.

"What was your first clue?" he said.

"It doesn't matter," she said.

"I can check into this Wool guy, but it doesn't seem like much of a lead. I'm fifty bucks a day, plus expenses."

She reached into her pocket and pulled out two twenties and a ten.

"Usually I ask for the money later."

He put it into his wallet and she stood to leave. He got her number in his notes and watched her climb into a blue gremlin. She popped back out carrying a large canvas painting. Rolfe took it from her and she sped away.

—

He took the painting back into his office and set it down on his couch. Rolfe picked up his phone and dialed. A moment later, a Brixton cop picked up. He didn't sound appreciative to be phoned by the detective.

"Hey, it's Edgar Rolfe."

"You're that p.i. right? What do you want?"

Rolfe knew by the voice it was Leonard Cake, a younger cop who was too new to already be talking dismissively.

"Yeah, that's me. Hey Cake, I have a question for you."

"Can you make it quick?"

"It's real quick. Was there a hit and run last night? Around the east side of town?"

"There was."

"And was it a bum who was killed?"

"It was."

"Any idea who did it?"

"Nope."

"Any interest in finding out?"

"We have better things to do."

"Any opposition in me finding out?"

"We won't pay you if that's what you mean."

"Someone already is. A relative of the deceased."

"Hold on a moment."

There was a silence on the phone. Rolfe could hear the receiver being put down and the shuffling of feet. He poured a small cup of coffee and had a few sips before he heard the cop return.

"Go for it. If someone is wasting their money to pay you then by all means."

"Isn't it a little unusual for you to approve of me solving a murder?"

"If you weren't you then maybe, but you stay out of our way for the most part. I can trust you know what to do."

"Yeah I think I do."

"You sound unsure, Rolfe. Were you looking for a way out of this case?"

"No, it's just a little out of my wheelhouse."

"Enjoy it. I'd be dying to get on a case like this. They keep me inside most of the time because I'm too green. I won't be out solving murders for at least another ten years if I'm lucky."

"Yeah, yeah. I'll call you when I have something."

Rolfe hung up, finished his coffee and headed to the gallery. It was in southern Brixton and the afternoon sun lit the place up with warmth. That and the young people who seemed to crowd the place. Rolfe was parked outside for ten minutes, watching them come and go. They were nearly all youths. Fresh, bright eyed faces wanting to see the latest offerings from Brixton's creatives. Three statues stood apart in front of the large concrete building. They were a Pegasus, a man with a sword, and a naked women showing it all for the passerby. *It doesn't look like the type of place where a murderer would hide.*

Rolfe had the painting in his passenger seat, glancing at it from time to time. It was an oil painting of what looked like a dog mixed with a barn. Colors were splashed together without any pattern. *I've seen kindergartners make better finger paintings than this.*

The dick hopped out of his car and into the gallery.

Rolfe was flooded with more color, statues, and art after stepping inside. The gallery wasn't filled, but there were plenty of people walking around and taking in the scenery. A man with long black hair approached the detective. He was short even when compared to the five-eight private eye in a black and tan suit. He walked towards Rolfe with an outstretched hand and a grin. *He definitely thinks I'm someone else. Just go with it, you damn fool. It might lead us somewhere.* Rolfe looked down at the hand before instinctively shaking.

"O'Strander, I'm so glad you made it. You're early too. That's a very good first impression you make. How was the ride over? Are you enjoying Brixton so far? Have you had any of our local cuisine?"

"Yeah, I'm having a great time so far. Thanks. I-"

"I know, you want to get right to it. Your assistant mentioned you're only here to talk business and that you don't waste time with chit chat."

A young full-lipped woman walked by and waved.

"See you later Mr. Wool," she said.

This is the guy that Keyes thinks hit her brother? He doesn't look like he'd kill anyone. I guess that's how they manage to pull it off. Hit a homeless guy at night then come in the next day with a smile.

"Sorry about that, let's get started."

Wool walked down a hall filled with water color and oil paintings on the walls. There were still lifes, naked men, busty women, and plenty of animals. They were nice too. Much nicer than the piece that was in the detective's car. Wool would throw his hands at the youths hanging in parts that he went. The gawkers moved on to another area of the gallery, allowing the two men to take in the paintings by themselves.

"I know your assistant said you prefer looking at them without an audience."

Rolfe nodded.

"Your assistant also said you were looking for something with horses."

Wool waved his hand again and sure enough there was a painting of a horse that could be considered half scale. The features were realistic, but the colors were fantastical. Blues made up the mane, oranges made up the hooves, everything in between was sprinkled in the fur.

"What do you think of this one?" said Wool.

Rolfe stared at the painting. He scratched his chin and shifted his nose.

"It's very nice. I like the artist's choice of colors."

"I knew that you would."

"Is this artist still with us?"

Wool shook his head.

"As you should already know, this one like most of the others here have passed."

"Is that the fate of all artists? To not be appreciated until it's too late?"

"I didn't know you thought of such things, Mr. O'Strander."

Rolfe scratched his chin once more.

"What happens to the ones who don't die in obscurity?"

"Well I suppose some of them enjoy the wealth of life."

"And others? What happens to them? What happens before they die? You ever think they become homeless?"

"I don't know. I'm not a welfare administrator."

Rolfe began pacing back and forth in front of the horse painting.

"I'm not sure about this one now. I'm thinking I need something hotter. Something cutting edge. Have you heard of this artist named Keyes?"

Rolfe watched the curator's face. It barely twitched at the mention of Keyes.

"I can't say that I have. Is it a local artist? What medium do they work with?"

"He was a local oil painter, yes."

"I was starting to think you weren't interested in the work of the deceased."

"Depends on the artist I suppose."

"I don't know of this artist, but if he's local then I'm sure I can find his work for you."

"I actually have a painting of his in my car. I could get it for you if you don't mind."

"Me, mind? Not at all. Please take your time."

Rolfe hurried back to his Chevy Vega and grabbed the painting from it. The barn dog mixture peered into his mind. *Who would pay for such a thing? Even worse, who would kill for this? I don't want to see this guy's other work if this is an example of what's on sale.*

The same woman from earlier passed by again still holding a friendly face. She was walking towards some friends lounging by the naked woman statue. *Is this what all the young people are doing these days? I guess it beats watching TV. At least someone is enjoying these dead artists. It's just a shame that they aren't alive to see it.*

Rolfe carried the painting back and found Wool where he left him. He was sitting on a bench in the middle of the gallery staring at the horse.

"It is a little overdone, isn't it?" he said.

"The horse? It's fine. Take a look at this."

Rolfe kept his attention on the curator's face once more. This time he did more than twitch. His face turned into a grimace, but only for a second as to not give away his true intentions except to those who were paying attention. Not that the detective would blame the man. The only joy this painting would bring is using it as kindling.

"What do you think of it?" said Rolfe.

"It's something. It's got a lot of character."

"And you've never seen anything like it before?"

"Nothing like this has ever been in my gallery. This is the artist you're interested in?"

"Well, yes. I find his work to be quite profound."

"That's one way to put it."

"You've really never seen this artist's work?"

"Mr. O'Strander I don't know why you'd think I'd lie about this."

"Maybe you have a reason. You know, like how people remain obscure before blowing up beyond their control?"

"I try to give my customer what they want. I wouldn't hide art from them. Is this really the type of painting you're looking for?"

The same large lipped woman returned again. Her smile had left her face. Now she was as still as the statues outside. She walked up to Wool and whispered in his ear. Wool looked up and down at the detective and cleared his throat.

"Please excuse me for a moment. I hope you don't mind, but something immediate has come up."

"I hope everything's okay."

"Absolutely. Hold on and we can continue our discussion."

Wool walked away with the young woman and left the detective alone holding the painting in front of the rainbow horse. *Everything's fine right? I'm sure he just had a phone call to take or something. A place like this must take a lot of phone calls.*

Another man soon came into view. He was taller than the dick with short white hair and a filled out body. He too approached Rolfe with a smile and outstretched hand like Wool had done earlier. *Oh, great, he probably thinks I'm this O'Strander too.*

"O'Strander? It's good to finally meet you. I've heard much about you."

Rolfe shook the hand.

"Thank you. May I ask who you are?"

The portly man gave a chuckle.

"It's the darnedest thing. You and I share the same name. It seems we share the same hobby of collecting art too."

The man broke the handshake with a cool shudder. Wool returned with disdain.

"I'm so sorry Mr. O'Strander. I don't know who this impostor is."

O'Strander grabbed Rolfe by the collar.

"It won't take long to find out. You one of those boys after my money?" said O'Strander.

Rolfe struggled to talk. Wool urged the real O'Strander to let the detective down. He cleared his throat. O'Strander wiped his hands on his pants as if touching the detective were enough to catch lymphoma. Rolfe looked to Wool for more support, but found none. That was the only mercy the curator would offer.

"Why would I pretend to be you if I wanted to steal your money?"

"I don't know why you criminal types do anything that you do."

"I think we're all a little confused here. I'm not a criminal."

"You better explain yourself quick mister. I have Betty waiting in the other room. I told her to phone the police if I'm not back in five minutes."

"And I'd like to know why you're pretending to be me."

"I'm not pretending to be you."

"Then what are you doing?"

Rolfe slowly reached into his pocket and pulled out his badge. He handed it to O'Strander who showed it to Wool who handed it back to the detective.

"You're a dick?"

"Private."

"I still don't understand. Why's a private eye pretending to be me?"

"I came in here and Wool thought I was you. I went with it to see what I could find out regarding my case."

"Well that doesn't make any sense. If you're a detective, why wouldn't you tell me that? I'd be sure to answer any questions you have," said Wool.

O'Strander started laughing, his belly jiggling as he did.

"Don't you understand? The dick here thinks you're up to no good. That about it?"

Rolfe nodded.

"Sorry to blow your cover then," said O'Strander.

"What did I do?" said Wool, "Why would anyone be wanting to put a tail on me?"

"I'm not sure. I think there's been a misunderstanding. A client wanted me to check you out is all."

O'Strander glanced at painting Rolfe was holding.

"What do you have in your hands there? You're not robbing the place while you're at it? Or were you hired to steal a painting and I blew your cover again?"

O'Strander chuckled more. He shook more than a jar of jelly on a dryer.

"No, it's one I brought myself. I was seeing if Wool here recognized it."

Rolfe briefly showed it to the white haired man before turning it away.

"Is that a Keyes?"

"You knew that from seeing a glimpse of it? It's not even signed."

O'Strander grabbed the painting from the detective, brought it close to his face and let the dog barn monstrosity overtake him. He returned it to Rolfe.

"That's a Keyes painting all right."

"You knew the artist? He apparently had been homeless before recently passing."

"He? No, Keyes is a woman. She was an old student of mine. Back when I still gave a damn about inspiring the next generation."

"Now I'm the one who's confused. You're telling me a woman named Keyes painted this?"

"Definitely. I recognize that horrendous style anywhere. She must have painted hundreds like this."

"Do you know what happened to her?"

"I've heard that she turned to the bottle after years of rejection. I don't blame her. I'd drink too if all I could paint were that. Who told you that a man painted this?"

She did of course. Wait a minute. I never even got the name of the victim. The damn woman didn't tell me her brother's name. Why wouldn't she? Unless she doesn't know.

"I'm not at liberty to say. I think I got what I came here for though. Thank you, O'Strander."

"I'm happy to have helped."

Rolfe headed towards the door. Wool stood in silence and O'Strander was still letting out the giggles. Rolfe turned back with a wave before leaving.

"Sorry for causing any confusion."

"You kidding me? That was the most I've laughed in a long time. You can use my name anytime."

The detective went straight to the payphone outside the gallery. He blew into his pocket whistle and dialed the number that Keyes gave him. It rang twice before she answered.

"Hello?"

Even now her greeting sounded slurred.

"This is Edgar Rolfe. I think I found something I should show you."

"What is it?"

"I'd rather wait to explain in person."

"I can meet you at your office. Give me a few minutes first."

"I think it'd be better for me to come to you. You sound like you've been spending the afternoon grieving with a couple drinks."

"Okay. I'll stay right here."

"I'm going to need your address."

"Oh, right."

The detective scribbled down the address and hung up the phone. *This is great. Look what you got yourself into now.*

He whistled once more into the receiver and dialed the police station. Leonard Cake picked up after three rings.

"Hello, Brixton police."

Rolfe held the phone still and didn't say a word.

"Please don't waste our time with prank calls. There's real people who need help out there."

Cake hung up and Rolfe followed the example. He climbed into his Vega and within fifteen minutes was outside Keyes' house. It looked as expected. Rundown, trash on the lawn, and an air of sadness that comes with a life of failure. Rolfe parked down the street and double backed on foot. The blue gremlin was in the driveway and something caught his eye when he walked by it.

The front was covered in a reddish brown substance. That wasn't all. A spiderweb crack was spreading on the left headlight. And there was a noticeable dent in the hood.

How didn't I see this before? What kind of detective am I?

He checked that his revolver was still in place before walking up the broken steps of the porch. He knocked on the screen door and there was no answer. Broken and empty bottles populated the deck. They seemed to be the only residents home. *Maybe I should find a phone and call it in.* He stepped back towards the stairs when he heard a sobbing sound coming from inside. He knocked once more with no reply and decided to go in uninvited.

The house looked about as nice as the outside. More trash, old newspapers, and broken glass made up the decor. A TV sat in the corner, turned on with the sound low, and only half tuned in. But the most defining feature were the paintings. There were indeed hundreds of the same mediocre style that Rolfe had seen in the first painting. The sobbing sound led Rolfe to the kitchen where he found Keyes sitting at a messy table. A bottle of whiskey and a pistol were her only company. The bottle was open for easy access and she took a swig before noticing the detective.

"Oh, it's you," she said.

"Yeah, it's me."

"What did you want to tell me? What did you find out?"

"Enough I'd suppose."

"Is that so?"

She drank more and Rolfe glanced down at the gun. He moved his hand closer to it, but was cut off by her words.

"Did you find proof that Wool was involved?"

"Nope, but I did find out who was."

She sipped again.

"Who?"

"I'm looking right at her."

"What are you talking about? I didn't kill my brother."

"Cut the bullshit, I know he wasn't your brother."

She nearly emptied the whiskey after hearing that. She grabbed the pistol, holding it limply in her hand. It was aimed at the detective's chest and he knew to keep still.

"I didn't mean to. It was an accident."

Rolfe took a half-step towards the drunken woman.

"If that's true then why didn't you stay and turn yourself in?"

"We all make mistakes, don't we?"

"Some larger than others and this one is pretty big. It'll continue to grow every minute you don't do the right thing."

She lifted the gun again at the detective and he matched the movement with his hand. He grabbed her wrist and squeezed it tight until she dropped the gun. He caught the pistol before it hit the ground and slipped it into his coat pocket. A quick jab into her face caused her to sober up. She jumped to her feet and swung the whiskey bottle at his head. She missed, letting it smash into the table before falling back into her chair.

"What exactly was your plan here? I'm still trying to wrap my head around what you were trying to do."

"I thought maybe Wool would get blamed and I'd be off the hook or maybe he'd like my art and it'd finally be in a gallery."

"So you didn't think this through?"

"I only hit that man last night and I was drunk. I haven't had much time to think."

"Maybe your head would be clearer if you laid off the booze. Not that it matters now. You'll have plenty of time to think where you're going."

"Could you at least let me permeate on a sentence that isn't so cliche?"

"Alright. How about this? Your art is bad and I say that knowing art is subjective. I'm sorry you turned to alcohol to deal with your failures. Still a man died because of your inability to at least be a drunk who doesn't drive. Should I continue or was that tailored enough to your lack of effort for a plan?"

She puffed out her chest and spit on the floor.

"What are you going to do with me?"

"I've got to call the cops and turn you in."

"Why would they believe you?"

"You mean why would they believe a private detective in their town who has only ever played by the rules?"

"Yes."

"Because your car is still painted with the blood of that poor man you killed. A man who's real name I realized I don't know and you didn't bother to make up. I should have gone down to the shelter and asked a few questions to the people there. I'm sure someone saw your drunk ass run over that man."

"I knew you wouldn't. For the same reasons the cops didn't look into this. You don't care about those bums either. You're only doing this under the guise of money."

"That might be true. At least I'm not out there running them over with my car."

"Please don't do this."

Rowlf pointed his finger at the woman.

"Don't make me tie you up."

"Can I have one last drink please?"

"You mean that wasn't your last bottle?"

"There's another in the fridge."

He granted her request, filling a small glass and leaving it on the table while he used her phone.

"Brixton police, how can I help you?"

"Leonard? It's Rolfe. I found the person who hit the bum last night."

"Already? Well where is he?"

"It's a she and I'm at her house."

Rolfe gave the address.

"You stay put and I'm going to want to know what the hell happened."

"Don't worry. We're not going anywhere."

The cops arrived a half hour later. Rolfe explained the story to a couple of cocked heads who were only as confused as he was. The detective offered to turn in the painting and money he was paid. Brixton's finest told him to keep it as a reward for a job well done. He shrugged off being treated like a child and tossed the painting back into his car.

—

Edgar Rolfe headed for the entrance of the Chinese restaurant. A customer was ahead of him, holding the door to let him in. The detective appreciated it as he was holding the painting in his arms. The customer grabbed their food, paid and left Rolfe alone with the Wus. Rolfe took a seat on the stool and laid the canvas on the counter.

"What's with the ugly painting?" said Bao.

"Apparently that woman who interrupted my lunch had painted it."

"It's hideous. Why would anyone paint that?"

"Let me see it," said Sun.

Rolfe lifted it for the cook to see and he was met with a grimace.

"You want it? I was thinking we can hang it down here."

"If you want to scare away the customers, sure," said Sun.

"That seems to be everyone's reaction, including mine."

"You want something to eat?"

"Absolutely."

"What exactly happened with the woman?" said Bao.

"She was the murderer."

"I knew she was a bit off from looking at her."

"Next time maybe you could give me a bit of that insight."

"If she's a murderer then why are you keeping that painting?"

"I don't know. Poor woman was so set on her art being seen that maybe I'll keep it to look at."

"As long as you keep it in your office," said Sun.

Bao shuddered then cracked up.

"You won't believe it. I just felt a little kick."

Sun stopped cooking and looked at her belly.

"I thought it was too early for it to be kicking."

"I guess I was wrong."

"I wish I could have recorded you saying that."

"Stop gloating and get over here."

Sun ran to his wife and gently felt her belly. He could feel the baby stirring inside and he was grinning ear to ear.

"Rolfe would you like to feel it?"

"You sure?"

"Get over here."

The detective got off his stool, sauntering over to the couple. He paused a step away from the woman.

"Okay, but it's 'uncle' Rolfe from now on."

Mobster Gumbo

Sal Corbucci stormed into the Club. He went straight past Fat Louie, the stripper with a lazy eye, and the two old men who were in there at 9 a.m. on a Wednesday. His family owned the Club and everyone in Brixton knew it. That's why they had the confidence to give it the name it has. The Corbuccis were the leading mafia family in town and no one would be able to bring them down.

Sal headed for the back office where he kicked open the door and slammed it behind him. Sitting at a table was his cousin Louie. Now this is a different Louie from the fat fuck who made sure the customers didn't get too rowdy. This one had some actual brains in him. He was sitting at the table checking the books before Sal interrupted him. He closed the folder and stared back at his cousin.

"You're in a mood already, I see," said Louie.

Sal sat down in the chair next to him as angry as someone could.

"You could say that," he said.

"You want me to ask what's wrong or are you merely getting out some anger?"

"No, sure, I'll say. You see we got a big fucking problem. My father's lighter is missing and if we don't get back before he gets back in town then we're in a hell of a lot of trouble."

"You mean you're in a lot of trouble."

"And if I am then who do you think I'm going to take it out on?"

Louie laughed and scratched his head.

"I'm guessing you want me to help you look for it, right?" said Louie.

"You're damn right I do," said Sal.

"Don't you think I have anything more important to do?" he said looking down at the folder.

"That can wait. Come on Louie, I'm only asking you because I know you can keep your mouth shut that it was lost at all."

Louie stood up, went to the fridge, and took out two lagers. He popped them both and handed one to Sal.

"Little early isn't it?" said Sal.

"I'm going to need if I'm spending my day helping you."

"Does that mean you're in?"

"You know I wouldn't let you down. Now tell me, when's the last time you had it?"

"That's another problem cause I never touch the damn thing. It's always in its case in his personal office. I stopped by his house last night and saw it was gone."

"How we do we know uncle Junior didn't take it on his trip?"

"Because he doesn't ever touch it either."

"What the fuck do you think happen to it then? Do you think someone stole it?"

"I don't what happened I only know we need to find it. Someone better not have stolen it. Cause whoever did is going to get their head cut off and mailed back to their mother."

A knock came at the door and in came their tall cousin, Ciro. Sal and Louie paid him no attention and continued their conversation. The walking scarecrow listened to his two cousins mumble about where the lighter could be. It took him a beer of his own to speak up.

"I think I fucked up"

"No one cares. We have bigger issues here."

"That's what I'm talking about. I took Sal Sr.'s lighter."

Sal jumped out of the chair and grabbed his younger cousin by the collar of the cheap blue suit was he was wearing.

"You lanky bastard. Where the fuck is it?"

"Yeah, I'm not about to give up that kind of information. I'm afraid what you'll do if I tell you."

"You should be afraid of what I'll do if you don't."

"Don't give me that bullshit. You won't hurt me, Sal. We're family."

"Yeah, you're right. That's why I'll have someone else do it for me."

—

Edgar Rolfe was still picking the crust from his eyes when he walked downstairs into the Chinese restaurant he lived on top of. Inside were Sun Wu and his wife pregnant wife, Bao.

"Hey you're starting to really show now," said Rolfe.

Sun shook his head at Rolfe. The detective tilted his slightly back.

"Yeah. So are you," said Bao.

"Hey I didn't mean to cause any offense."

"Me either. But I can tell your pants have been looking tighter lately. Do we need to cut off your potsticker supply?"

Rolfe let out a soft chuckle.

"I don't know what you're talking about. I've barely gained any weight."

"That's not what it looks like. Right Sun?"

"I'd prefer if you two kept me out of this."

Rolfe looked at the cook again. Sun shrugged his shoulders and the detective could pick up on what he saying. *Why'd you have to open your mouth at all?*

"Okay maybe I gained ten or fifteen pounds. It's barely noticeable."

"If you don't mind then I don't. It's your life Edgar. All I know is I'll lose my extra weight after the baby."

"You really think I packed on the pounds?"

"I'm only being honest with you unlike my husband over there."

Rolfe straightened himself and brushed the sides of his tan buttoned shirt.

"Fine I'm going for a jog then. Right now."

"Right now? What about your breakfast? Aren't you going to be hungry if you go five minutes without eating?" said Bao.

"I don't need any more extra calories."

"Oh come on Rolfe. She's only joking. That's what families do, they kid around. Stay and eat. Read the paper," said Sun.

"I will soon as I get back from treading a few miles."

The detective slipped out of the restaurant and back into his office upstairs. He had to dig through his closet to find his workout attire under his winter gear. His office may have become covered in clothes, but now wasn't the time to clean. He tossed off the suit he was wearing, jumped into a plain gray shirt and blue gym shorts before lacing up a pair of beat up sneakers.

Rolfe went back downstairs and stretched in the Chinese restaurant.

"See? My old workout clothes still fit fine. I'll be back in an hour or so."

"Be careful," said Sun.

"What do you think is going to happen to me out there?"

"He's right. You don't want to get hit by a car," said Bao.

"I'm not going to get hit by a car," said Rolfe.

The detective dashed out the door.

—

Rolfe had sprinted out the door and maintained that speed for twenty seconds. He looked back to make sure he wasn't in view of the restaurant before dropping to a panting state. That lasted a minute and he was still breathing heavily while slowly walking down the sidewalks of Brixton. *Maybe I have got a bit out of shape.* His stomach grumbled and his nose sniffed the morning air. *I've been sleeping in later too.*

It's time to make some changes. But maybe that can wait until I go back and get some food in me. I need some fuel if I'm going to keep running. He continued down the sidewalk and barely heard the black car pull up beside him.

He stopped his walk to see three men jumping out of the sedan. They looked familiar somehow. At least one of them did. *Where I do know these guys from?*

"Get him!"

A large lanky man went for the detective. Rolfe threw up his hands in defense, slugging the young man in the cheek. The other two men started laughing while the young one screamed for them to help him.

Rolfe planted his feet and swung at the shorter man. He easily ducked and swung back, knocking the dick to the ground. Rolfe took a deep breath before seeing a hood being placed over his head and feeling his body being ushered into the car. His kicks and flailing arms did little to prevent the men from taking him away from his new morning run routine. Those extra pounds would have to wait.

—

He could tell they were driving somewhere, but no clue why they'd want to bring him anywhere. *Did I piss someone off? No one more than usual. Why would they come for me so early too? Just keep calm, if they wanted you dead, you'd already be in heaven with the missus. She ain't ready for you and these guys clearly aren't bringing you there.*

Rolfe let his thoughts subside as the car came to a halt. He was ushered out of his and up a flight of stairs. He heard a door smash open and the hood was pulled off his head. He looked around and found himself in his own office. The three men were pacing around and Rolfe had been plopped onto his pull out bed. It clicked on who the fuck they were.

"Sal Corbucci, it's been a while," said Rolfe.

Sal turned from examining an empty fish tank and smiled.

"That's right, Eddie. Figure we could use your help again," said Sal.

"And who might the other two be? Two more members of the Corbucci family, I imagine?"

"You imagine right. The gangly one is Ciro and the other is Louie."

"I'd say I'm pleased to meet you, but considering you punched me, dragged me into a car, and broke down my door, I'm far from pleased right now."

A series of stomping sounds came from the stairs outside. Rolfe could hear the clicking of a shotgun and saw Sun holding it towards the mobsters. The mobsters in turn pulled out their own handguns.

"You okay up here Edgar?" said Sun.

"I'm not sure. Am I, Sal?"

"He's perfectly safe. Call him off, Rolfe," said Sal.

"I don't know. I don't feel safe."

"If we wanted you dead, you would be. We need your help," said Louie.

"Looks like they're customers, Sun," said Rolfe.

Sun Wu lowered the shotgun and turned back to go downstairs to his restaurant.

"They better replace this door cause I'm not doing it," he said.

"You heard him," said Rolfe.

"We'll take care of the door," said Louie.

The detective stood and took his place behind his desk while the mobsters still cased the office.

"Normally customers knock on the door, not knock me out."

Sal cleared his throat and took a seat in front of the desk.

"Yeah well, we didn't think you'd be willing to take us on as clients."

"Depends on what you need done. I try not to judge. This ain't exactly the first time you've needed my help now, is it, Sal?"

"This one is a little different than tracking someone for me."

"Cut to it then. Let me guess. You want me to dig up dirt on a rival family?"

Louie had poured Sal a cup of day old coffee and the mobster sipped it.

"I need you to help us find a lighter. It's the old man's. It's silver with gold trimming and it has a wolf engraved on it."

Rolfe took out his notepad and started scribbling.

"Why would you come to me? I'm not much of a cat burglar."

"We heard you were. Besides, we'd be looking for it together, as a family. Don't you get things back for people?" said Sal.

"Sure. Usually those are incapable of doing so themselves. Not people who want me to come along for the hell of it"

"This is reminding me of one of those Marlowe books. He was paid to go along for the ride," said Louie.

"And I'm guessing you didn't finish it," said Rolfe.

"Enough of this. You two can continue your book club another time. Are you interested or not? Cause we're gonna have a problem if not. Considering we already told you and all," said Sal.

"What could i possibly do with this information? I don't give a damn about some small town mobsters."

"We'll pay triple your normal rate. God knows you need it. I wouldn't let my kid live in a dump like this."

"You don't have any kids, Louie."

"Not yet. But we're trying and I imagine it breaks Eddie's parents hearts knowing he ended up like this."

Rolfe stopped scribbling in his notepad and cracked his fingers.

"Fine. I'll help you out. Now let's start with an easy question. Do you have any idea where this lighter could be?"

Sal and Louie looked at each other and chuckled.

"We know who knows except the dumb motherfucker doesn't want to tell us where the fuck it's at. We screamed at him and got nothing. We're hoping you might be able to get something from him," said Sal.

"Where is this guy now?"

"He's right here. Ciro is the dumb fuck in question. Aren't you Ciro?" said Louie.

The tall young man nodded his head.

"You're telling me that one of you knew where it is, but instead you decided to kidnap me and do what exactly?"

"The kidnap word is a little strong, don't you think?"

Rolfe reached into his desk and pulled out the Whitney pistol he kept there. He pointed it at Ciro's chest. Louie went to draw his own handgun, but Sal put a hand up to stop him.

"How about you tell me where the fuck you took the lighter and we can all move on with our lives?" said Rolfe.

Ciro swallowed and looked at his cousins before answering.

"I lost it," said Ciro.

"Where did you lose it. You have any room for brains in that stick you call a body?" said Sal.

"Tell him not to yell at me," said Ciro.

"I'm not telling him shit. Where is the goddamn lighter?" said Rolfe.

"It's at the zoo."

"Why the fuck is it at the zoo? Why the fuck were you even at the zoo?" said Louie.

"I was there with Winnie. I wanted to impress her."

"So you took the lighter that belongs the head of our family and you lost it there? Good going," said Sal.

"I didn't mean to lose it. I'm sure I'll find if I head there now."

"How about we go along with you to make sure you find it?" said Sal.

Rolfe lowered his Whitney and closed the notepad.

"Looks like we're all done here. How about you three get the fuck out of my office? I'll send a bill for the door to the Club."

Sal sipped from the cold coffee again.

"You're not getting out of this that easily, Eddie. You're coming along with us. We're doing this Marlowe style, right Louie?"

"That's right, cus."

"Fine, but let me at least get dressed first. I know I don't have a door anymore, but I'd like a little privacy."

"Yeah, fine. We'll be waiting down by your car," said Louie.

"My car?"

"We're paying you, so you're driving," said Sal.

The three Corbuccis shuffled out the door. Rolfe changed into his tan and black suit, checked his revolver in the holster and found the mobsters lounging around his green '71 Chevy Vega hatchback.

The youngest Corbucci had his hand in a bag of potato chips. Rolfe looked him in the eyes and grabbed the bag. He crumpled it and tossed it into a trash can that was outside the Wu's restaurant.

"No eating in the car," said Rolfe.

"You're a dick. All you guys do is eat in cars," said Ciro.

"Not me. If your car is a mess then so is the rest of your life."

"Guess that doesn't hold to offices, huh?" said Louie.

"Enough talking shit. If he doesn't want us to eat in his car then we aren't going to eat in his car. You've already fucked up enough, haven't you Ciro?" said Sal.

—

Being packed into a small car with three Italian-American men has more downsides than up. The first being the smell. Rolfe nearly screamed at them for eating the car when he explicitly said not to, but he looked around and none of them were eating. That hoagie smell of onions, rotting deli meat, and pickles were the natural odor the Corbucci men carried. *How are some of these guys married?* He turned to Sal who only grinned and waved his arms in directions for Rolfe to turn. Not that Rolfe didn't know how to get to the zoo, he did, but Sal insisted on going a route less traveled. *Why the fuck did I drive again then? That's another for the downside column.*

The Brixton Zoo was one the north side of town. It was built in the 50s as a post World War II idea to help bring tourists to town. Unfortunately it didn't work too well. The Philadelphia Zoo put the Brixton one to shame. No one wants to come see a few lions, a black bear, and a pack of wolves in Brixton when you can see elephants, giraffes, and tigers in Philly. And those who were already in south Jersey preferred going to the Cape May Zoo as a part of their day at the beach.

The Brixton Zoo survived on those already in town and those dumb enough to visit those who lived in town. Rolfe himself hadn't been there since he went on his first date with his first wife.

Rolfe parked his car in the small parking lot and the four men jumped out. Ciro took a deep breath of air as he stretched his long legs. Louie smacked him across the back of his head.

"Stop acting like a child. It was hardly a fifteen minute ride," said Louie.

"I can't help it that my legs get cramped. Don't be upset that God blessed me with my stature," said Ciro.

Louie smacked him again. Ciro raised his hand in defense, but Sal grabbed it and lowered it to his side.

"We don't have time for this shit. Both of you need to get along. Don't embarrass me in front of the detective," said Sal.

"We ain't embarrassing no one, are we Louie?" said Ciro.

"I don't think so, but you wouldn't know even if you were," said Louie.

Ciro went to smack Louie again and Sal barked at him.

"I said, enough already. Can you handle that or are you going to have to wait in the car?" said Sal.

Ciro looked to Rolfe who shook his head at him.

"Yeah, fine, Sal," said Ciro.

The men bought four tickets from a cute girl at the gates to the zoo. They headed in and already the zoo enraptured them. A cage of spider monkeys who were barely hopping around were directly to their left when they walked in. Across from that were two parrots not budging from their perches. To say the zoo was empty would be an understatement. There were the four men, the ticket girl, and maybe three others walking around the place.

"The fuck you come here for anyway? You really thought taking a girl to see a bunch of animals in cages would be the best way to get yourself laid?" said Sal.

"Sad animals at that," said Louie.

"Women always love it when I bring them here," said Ciro, "It's not my fault you two are stuck with your wives."

"Don't you dare imply there's something wrong with my wife," said Sal.

"I'm with Sal. At least we can stick to one unlike you dipping that dick in anything that takes it," said Louie.

"Do all you three do is bicker over everything you say?" said Rolfe.

"Sometimes we shoot wiseguys too," said Sal, "You feeling wise?"

"I'm rethinking that considering I agreed to come along for this shit. Now how about we get this over with? Where do you last remember having the lighter Ciro?"

Ciro looked at his feet which were miles away from his eyes before craning his head to upward to scan his surroundings. Monkeys, parrots, a single alligator in an enclosed pond, the lions. Where had he gone?

"We were all over. I don't remember when I lost it," said Ciro.

"That's great, are you even sure you lost it here?" said Rolfe.

"Well I knew I had it coming in. I smoked by the wolves. Those fuckers love watching people smoke. Then I remember not having it at the Black Country Rock diner later that afternoon."

"You went that long without smoking?"

Rolfe paced around the mobsters.

"Turns out the girl didn't like smoking so I waited. Does that matter?"

"It does. It lets me know that's probably the last time you had the lighter out of your pocket. Better that than thinking it was in your car this whole time," said Rolfe.

"So we should go to the wolves then?" said Ciro.

"You two go ahead. Louie and I are going to check out the gator. He's the same damn one that was here when I was a kid, I swear," said Sal.

"You're out of your damn mind if you think it's the same one," said Louie.

"See? You think you have all the brains in the family, but you don't even know that gators live a long time," said Sal.

"I just don't think it's plausible that this is the same one," said Louie.

Rolfe and Ciro walked away from the two men and they could still hear their argument fading away with each step.

The wolves were at the tail end of the zoo. They were out roaming in an enclosed space with fake cliffs and real trees scattered throughout it. Rails were put up along the exhibit. Ciro leaned on one while Rolfe looked around.

"I was right here, like this," said Ciro.

"You sure it didn't fall in?" said Rolfe.

"I'm pretty damn sure, but who knows?"

"I need you to think about this."

"Why do you care so much?"

"Because your cousin is paying me four times my going rate."

"That's all?"

"The sooner I find this lighter, the sooner I get away from you insane wops. The less time inhaling your smell, the better."

"Okay well I've got to tell you something, but you can't get mad."

Rolfe's ears perked up and he strained his head looking the tall man in the eyes.

"You know where it is, don't you?" said Rolfe.

"I do."

"Spill it then."

Ciro got off the railing and paced around as the wolves mimic'd his behavior behind him.

"That girl and I, we were at a protest here yesterday."

"I didn't take you for the type. What were you protesting?"

"Big oil or some shit like that. You're right, I'm not the type, but I can fake it for the right girl. Trust me, you would have done the same if you saw the tits on this girl."

"Get to the part about the lighter."

"Security ushered us out and patted us all down to make sure we had no weapons."

"And they took the lighter?"

Ciro nodded his head and it nearly fell off.

"Why didn't you say so?" said Rolfe.

"Sal and Louie would never let me hear the end of it if they found out. You're not going to tell them, are you?"

"Not if we can get the lighter back before they find out."

Rolfe started walking to the security building. They passed it on the way coming in and it hadn't changed its location since the zoo opened.

"What's security like here anyway? I figured a skyscraper like you could handle himself," said Rolfe.

"They got a big guy working here, not the type you want to get into a fight with while on a date, plus it was more romantic to get thrown out in protest. You've got to work the ladies, you know what I mean?"

"Can't say that I do."

They reached the small concrete building with parted blinds in the windows. It sat right in front of the lion's exhibit. *Probably the best way to catch those who were dumb enough to mess with the kings and queens of the jungle.* The two took a peek at them and they were sleeping on long flat rocks and in tall grass. They went back towards the security office and Rolfe crouched down to peek through the blinded window It looked like a standard guard outpost. There was a large radio receiver, a desk, file cabinets, and even a small cell in the there. *I didn't think they had the authority to actually hold people. Maybe those too drunk that they need the police to get rid of?* He saw boxes of crap on the floor that were labeled "Lost and Found." He more importantly saw that the place was empty of any guards.

"Looks like we're in the clear to go in," said Rolfe.

"You think it's in there?" said Ciro.

"We better hope so for your sake."

Rolfe jiggled the door handle and it was open. He and Ciro walked in to find it still empty. Rolfe dug through the box of found crap while the mobster paced around the place. He pulled out baseball cards, toy whistles, stuffed animals, and a couple cameras, but there was no lighter to be found.

"You find it yet?" said Ciro.

"What do you think?"

"You better hurry it up before the guard gets back."

Rolfe dumped the box on the desk. *I don't care if we're caught as long as we get the damn lighter and I can go home.*

The rest of the box was the same. Toys, small personal belongings, and no lighter.

"It's not in here Ciro."

Ciro looked at the pile of crap and tossed a teddy bear against the wall.

"What the fuck am I going to tell Sal?"

"I don't know, but we need to get out of here before the guard gets back," said Rolfe.

Ciro nodded and they walked out of the office. Rolfe felt himself lifting high into the air and his instinct was to thrust his elbow into whoever had grabbed him. *No way I'm getting sucker punched twice in one day.* He heard a groan and regained his footing. Rolfe turned to see the ambusher. He was big. He was grey. He had a nose jutting out that could cut marble. *He was Bruno?* His large frame was being stuffed into a standard beige zoo security uniform complete with a pocket radio transmitter and baton at his side. *I thought this zoo didn't have rhinos in it?*

Bruno had got his good look of the detective as well. The dick was still small and just as spunky.

"I didn't expect to see you again for a while, muppet," he said.

"Likewise. Today's full of unexpected and unwanted reunions," said Rolfe.

"Sorry about the grab, I didn't know who was rooting through the office."

"You alright from me jabbing your stomach?"

"I've been hit worse."

Ciro in the meantime had only been watching the interaction, but Rolfe caught enough glimpse of him to see that the olive color had faded from his face.

"You know this guy, Eddie? You two friends or something?" said Ciro.

"I wouldn't call us friends, but we've certainly met before. This the guy that took the lighter from you?"

"Yeah that's the asshole."

Bruno didn't have to glance at Ciro twice to know who he was.

"Oh you're back again, are you? Yesterday wasn't enough?"

"I've come back for what's mine," said Ciro.

"Is that why you brought a dick along with you?" said Bruno.

"I didn't exactly volunteer for the job, but yeah. That's why I'm here."

Bruno puffed his heavy chest out and laughed.

"I don't know what line of bullshit he's feeding you, but I didn't take anything from him."

"Oh yeah, what do you call having his lighter then?"

"I call it a tall man with a stacked girl who didn't want the cops to arrest them so he bribed me with a lighter he claimed was worth a lot of money. Damn thing is barely worth using for smoking. It can't hold a flame for shit."

"It's a decorative lighter," said Ciro, "And I need it back."

"You heard him, Bruno. How about you hand it over?" said Rolfe.

Bruno took the lighter out from his pocket. Rolfe looked to Ciro to confirm it was the right one and the mobster nodded.

"I've got no beef with you muppet. You helped me stay out of jail, but that can only go so far. This guy is a troublemaker."

Bruno was tossing the lighter gently in his hand and catching it in a continuous cycle. Ciro's eyes were locked on it as if he were going to snatch a rabbit from a starving dog's jaws.

"He said he was protesting something with his girl," said Rolfe.

"If you call throwing peanuts at the alligator, protesting then sure."

"You lied about that too?" said Rolfe.

"I couldn't tell you the truth. Plus I figured you were one of those bleeding heart types," said Ciro.

"How about you give the lighter back and we'll get out of your hair. Deal?"

"Alright muppet, it's all yours."

Rolfe could see it happen in slow motion. The lighter left the rhino's hands and went right over the mobster's head. Ciro didn't even attempt to raise his hands. It cleared the tall man completely and landed inside the nearest exhibit. And it wasn't the petting zoo with the goats and ducks. Instead it landed on a flat rock in the den of five sleeping lions. Ciro's brow furrowed and he screamed at Bruno.

"What the hell did you do?" said Ciro.

"Me? What the fuck is wrong with you, can't you catch?" said Bruno.

"You didn't give me a heads up or nothing."

"Who needs a heads up from this close? Oh well, looks like it's gone now."

"We have to go in there and get it," said Ciro.

"You out of your goddamn mind? No one is going in there."

"Bruno, do you know who this guy is?" said Rolfe.

"No and I'm real tired of him already."

"He's a Corbucci."

The guard scratched his head and it gave him no answers.

"That a new type of pasta or something?"

"No, that's the crime family that runs things in Brixton. I thought you'd know given our last adventure together."

"Hey, I'm no damn criminal. I'm trying to do honest work here. I don't keeps tabs on the local mafia."

"You hear of the Club?"

"Who hasn't?"

"They own it."

Bruno got the answers he needed from hearing that. He clutched at his baton in instinct.

"That doesn't change the fact that the lighter is in a lion's den, muppet, now does it?"

"A literal lion's den at that," said Rolfe.

"That's what I said."

Ciro was already near the railing with one leg over it.

"What are you doing?" said Rolfe.

"What's it look like? I'm going to get the lighter."

Bruno grabbed Ciro and pulled him off the lighter. Ciro threw a punch at the guard and the rhino returned the favor. The sound of footsteps headed their way. It was Sal and Louie running full sprint towards the scuffle. Sal had his pistol drawn and aimed at Bruno. Bruno had Ciro in a headlock while the skinny man was kicking his feet trying to get free.

"Alright, let him go," said Sal.

Bruno did as he was told and Sal kept his gun aimed at him.

"Lower your gun, Sal," said Rolfe.

Sal steadied the pistol.

"What's this fat fuck doing to my cousin?" said Sal.

"He was stopping him from jumping in with those lions," said Rolfe.

Sal lowered his gun a little, holding it limp in his hands.

"Why the fuck were you trying to go in with the lions, Ciro?"

"Cause that's where this crazy bastard threw your father's lighter."

Sal brought the gun back up again. Rolfe slowly put himself between the pistol and Bruno.

"Out of the way, Eddie," said Louie from the side.

"Your cousin here keeps spinning tales to get himself out of the fire."

"Is that so?" said Sal.

"Yeah. Now put that gun away unless you're in the mood to do something real stupid that you'll regret. Because that's what I'm about to do."

Sal shifted the pistol back into his coat pocket. Rolfe could see Bruno breath a deep sigh of relief. That's when he took the window of opportunity. The detective flung himself over the railing and slid down the concrete wall landing feet first in the lion's den. He looked up to see the Corbuccis' and Bruno's eyes grow wide. He returned his gaze to his level surroundings. He could see all five lions scattered around sleeping. The lighter was sitting on a rock about twenty feet away with only one sleeping lion by it.

There was a door on the far wall which Rolfe prayed would be unlocked. He slowly stepped through the grass. A lion was close enough to him that he could see it breathing. He held in his own breath in respect and didn't even want the sound of exhaling to stir their slumber. He passed another lion, watched as its paw twitched, and kept going. The lighter was within his reach and the detective quickly snagged and held it up to the men above.

Ciro let out a loud cheer.

Sal had tried to cover his cousin's mouth, but it got out anyway.

The lions' eyes cracked open, their noses smelled the air, and their heads cocked at Rolfe. He bolted for the door.

The detective didn't have to look back to know the lions were following him. They weren't running, but instead taking their time. This would be an easy meal.

His hand grabbed the door knob and jiggled it. It wouldn't budge. *Why would anyone lock this? Do they think the lions could open it.*

Rolfe looked up to the men and saw Bruno was no longer among them. *Hopefully getting a tranq gun or a real one or something. What happened to the trigger happy Sal?*

The lions were gaining ground on him now. Slowly encircling him on all sides with the door to his back. The maned lion let out a yawn and Rolfe had a front seat view to his pointed fangs. *This is your own fault you know. No one told you to jump in here. Wait a minute, how dumb can you be? You've got your own heat.*

He searched his own jacket pocket for his revolver and held it at the lions who didn't understand what it meant. *Do I really want to kill a lion though? Kill or be killed I guess. I don't think you'll be winning any fans over with this one, Rolfe.*

He pulled the hammer back and heard a loud bang, but it wasn't the sound of his gun. It was the Corbucci men. Sal shot his gun off into the air. Louie and Ciro were pounding on the railing and shouting into the air. The lions turned away from Rolfe and headed to check out the sounds for themselves. A tear escaped the detective's cheek and he holstered his revolver. He leaned back on the door and nearly fell. It had opened on account of Bruno being there. Rolfe nearly hugged the man, but instead bolted through and slammed the door behind him.

"That's the most insane thing I've ever seen someone do. What do you they have on you? Pics of you with someone who isn't your missus? Proof that you killed the wrong guy?" said Bruno.

"Nothing."

"Man, that makes it even worse. You're lucky those sons of bitches didn't tear you apart."

"I think most of them were women."

"Daughters of bitches then. Come on, let's get you back upside."

The two went back up and Rolfe immediately put the lighter in Sal's hand.

"That was some good work, Eddie. How about we bump that two hundred bucks up to two thousand?" said Sal.

"No thanks. I don't want to feel like I owe you something."

"You're a clever guy, Rolfe," said Louie.

"I'm only trying to stay alive long enough to die at old age."

"You had me fooled when you jumped into a pit of lions," said Ciro.

"I'll still pass. Besides who knows if I ever get hired to steal this lighter from your family."

"You're joking right?" said Sal.

"You never know."

"Then let's say this. If you're ever against the Corbuccis we promise not to shoot you immediately. We'll give you a thirty second head start."

"Man that's much better than two thousand dollars."

—

The Corbuccis parted ways as soon as Rolfe got back to his office. The detective pocketed the cash payment and stomped into Wu's restaurant. Sun was in the kitchen and came out when he heard the detective slump in a stool.

"Hey thanks for the back up this morning. It's nice knowing I can count on you when I need to," said Rolfe.

"Don't mention it. I couldn't let anything happen to uncle Rolfe, right? You hungry? How about some dinner?"

"That's a big yes from me."

"You look like you could use it. I'm guessing you got some cardio in hanging with those greaseballs today. They do something to get your heart racing?"

"More than you know. I've got a great one to tell you tonight."

Meets Halloween Jack

Octobers in Brixton, New Jersey are mostly calm, quiet, and usually peaceful. The town is settling down after the warm summer and enjoying the brisk weather that has arrived with the fall. But then of course there's Halloween. The one day a year where people get to be someone else for a change while getting drunk and stuffing their faces full of sugar. The Brixton populace loved Halloween and this year would be no different. It was the morning of October 30th and the streets were well decorated by now. Ghosts hung from lamps, carved pumpkins haunted doorsteps, and skeletons were peeking through curtained windows. Children could barely contain themselves in their classrooms as they thought of this year's trick or treat route for their best potential bounty of candy.

Every town loves Halloween though, doesn't it? What made this one so special? Well Brixton had their own local celebrity who heralded the holiday all year round. Halloween Jack was his name and he ran a weekly television show out of the BRTV station in the center of town. You know the type; cheesy old horror movies, silly in between segments on cheap sets, and the budget to go along with it.

Jack was there now in the BRTV station, sitting at the desk in his office, scribbling down ideas for tomorrow night's Halloween special. His office wasn't like his "spooky" set. It was plain, but that's to be expected when your onscreen life is surrounded by the macabre. He was in a drab gray suit with no tie and he wouldn't need to put one on for at least an hour or two. No one else in his section was in this early at the station besides the TV host.

He stared at the notepad and what he had so far. His scribbles amounted to nothing more than a doodle of a skeleton holding a pumpkin. *Maybe I need some coffee to get the brain juices flowing.* He went out to the kitchenette, poured himself a mug of black caffeine and headed back to his office. But he was no longer alone. He could see someone was standing in there. They were bent over, wearing a brown hooded sweatshirt, and rooting through Jack's desk. The host clenched his fist and stepped inside.

"What are you doing in my office?"

The hood stood and it was clearly a man by his broad build, but his identity was concealed. He wearing a skull mask with sunglasses over his face. Jack steadied himself and cleared his throat.

"You know, Halloween isn't until tomorrow."

"Of course you'd know that, wouldn't you Halloween Jack? Let's just say I like starting early."

Jack looked around his office, but there wasn't much to aid him in a fight. All the good objects; lamp, chair, even the pens were all near the intruder. Jack couldn't help but scrunch his nose. Whoever was in his office smelled. Not just smelled, but stunk like a deli with a broken refrigerator. The sooner he was out of here the better.

"Can I help you with something?" said Jack.

"How kind of you to ask," said the skull-man, "I'm looking for a blue gem. You know where I can find one around here?"

The skull-man's voice was a snarl. Jack dug his fingernails into his palms.

"Can't say that I know what you're talking about."

"That's strange cause I could have sworn that you'd know. See I heard that you knew and my information guy is highly reliable. Or are you saying that he was lying? Is that it?"

"I don't know you or your intel man, man. I don't know anything about a gem."

The skull-man let out a laugh as he pulled out a pistol.

"Maybe this will jog that memory of yours. You think you know now?"

Jack charged the skull-man, kicking up his desk and sending it into the intruder, knocking him on his ass as paper and pencils scattered in the air. Luckily the pistol went along with it and Halloween Jack grabbed it before standing over the thief. The skull-man was still shaken from the fall when his own gun was aimed at him.

"Who the hell told you about the gem?" said Jack.

"I'm not telling you shit."

"You can either tell me or the cops. Either way I'm going to find out."

"Nah, I don't think so."

"Why are you so confident? You have a suicide tablet? Are you really willing to die over not telling me?"

"No, it's not that."

The sound of footsteps thudding into the room rang through Jack's ears.

The TV host turned to see another two brown hooded figures wearing masks and sunglasses. One was in a witch mask and the other wore a pumpkin. That wasn't the problem though. The problem was that they too were holding a gun aimed at Jack's chest. And they too lacked the practice of proper hygiene just like their skull-faced friend.

"Give us the gun or you'll be getting some lead for breakfast," said the pumpkin-man.

Jack did as he was told, handing over the pistol with a scowl.

"It's real good to see you two right now," said the skull-man.

"We were wondering what was taking you so long," said the witch-man.

The skull-man was helped to his feet by the witch and the three men all held their guns at the host.

"I didn't expect him to be here so early," said the skull-man, "But it might be some good fortune cause I can't seem to find the damn thing."

"And let me guess, he isn't willing to help you on this scavenger hunt?" said the pumpkin-man.

The skull-man nodded. The pumpkin-man jabbed Jack in the stomach and the host staggered.

"You have no idea what you're after," said Jack.

"Cut the crap. Where's the fucking gem and don't give us any more bullshit," said the pumpkin-man.

"We don't want to shoot you man, but we will," said the witch-man.

Jack could hear no others on his floor in the building. His office was in disarray from both the intruders and his own kicking, but there was nothing left to help him in the fight against three men with guns all marking him. He let out a sigh and reached into his jacket pocket. He pulled out a blue gem the size of an apple and looked down at it. It was a light blue and he could see it was starting to slowly glow. He glanced at it one last time before tossing it to the masked thieves.

The skull-man caught it and the thieves dashed out the door to the elevator.

-

Halloween for private eye Edgar Rolfe meant settling in with a bowl of candy and watching whatever Halloween Jack put on for his horror movie marathon. It meant handing out candy to kids in their costumes and eyeing their mothers while they did so. But today was the 30th and it meant lugging his tired body off his futon bed and getting dressed. It was already 9 a.m. and he still hadn't made himself decent for the day.

His latest case ended with a whimper. A woman was cheating on her husband and he got the pictures to him to prove it. But the woman came clean before he could hand the pictures over and the husband felt he didn't need to pay full amount for the dick's services. Luckily Rolfe didn't need to use his revolver to encourage his pay. Instead the dutiful wife paid the share with an extra fifty on top for the trouble. The tip made the detective feel comfortable enough to sleep in.

Edgar Rolfe tossed on his black and tan suit and headed downstairs to the Chinese restaurant. He could hear the owners chatting before he opened the door. The cook, Sun

Wu, and his pregnant wife, Bao were sitting in the seating area that greeted customers.

"Hey there uncle Rolfe, how's your morning going?" said Sun.

Rolfe was still picking the crud out from his eyes, but he smiled all the same.

"Going fine, how's my favorite couple?"

"Doing better now that you're here," said Bao.

"Why's that? You two having a fight or something?"

"More like we need to ask you something," said Sun.

Rolfe took a seat on a stool by a counter.

"This about me being late on the rent? If so it just so happens that I have a few extra bucks I could cough up," he said.

Both of the Wus chuckled.

"No, well, not this time it isn't," said Sun.

Rolfe let himself breathe and he helped himself to some coffee while nodding to let them know he was still listening.

"What is it then?"

Bao cleared her throat and rested her hands softly on her plump belly.

"We were wondering if you'd drive me when it's time to have the baby," she said.

Rolfe nearly choked on the hot coffee. He coughed out some droplets that fell onto his shirt.

"You want me to drive?"

"Would that be a problem?" said Sun.

"Normally no, but my car has been acting up lately. I don't know if it'd be safe."

"You could always drive our car," said Bao.

Rolfe took another sip and nearly opened his mouth to respond when they all heard a scream come from outside.

"Go on, check it out," said Bao.

"Look you know you can count on me if you need a driver, alright?" said Rolfe rushing towards the door.

He opened it to find a familiar face screaming at the sky. It wasn't a face that he knew personally. Only one he watched every week he could. One he could recognize even if it wasn't in his costume.

"Halloween Jack?" said Rolfe.

Jack's face was flushed, he looked like he had been drenched in sweat then dried then drenched again. He glared at the detective.

"Yeah, that's me," he said.

"Are you okay? Why are you out here screaming in the streets?"

"I'm fine, nothing for you to get worry about."

"You sure? You don't sound fine. I'm a big fan by the way."

"Of course you are. Everyone says that around here."

"I mean it. I watch every show I can. I especially love the Saturday night monster-thons."

Halloween Jack looked at the detective.

"What do you want from me? An autograph or something?"

"Jack, you sure you're okay? You were out here yelling. I just want to help."

"I don't think anyone can help me with my problem."

"Is this about what movies to pick for tomorrow? May I suggest Them! or the Horror of Dracula?"

Jack shook his head. His lip nearly fell off from quivering before he snapped it back into place.

"What is it then? My name is Edgar Rolfe. I'm a private detective. There's got to be some way I can help you. Come on, follow me up into my office right here."

Rolfe headed up the stairs, turned his head to see the host was still standing in the street. Rolfe waved at him, and Jack started slowly following up the steps, and they both went inside.

Jack took a seat in front of the desk, Rolfe poured himself more coffee, and poured one more for his newfound client. The detective took his seat, pulled out his notepad and held his pen firmly.

"So why are you here today?" said Rolfe.

"Me? You're the one who dragged me up here."

"Oh, right. Well if it isn't about your job then what's causing your meltdown? Love life down the drain? Someone you know gone missing? Something irreplaceable stolen from you?"

Halloween Jack tapped on the desk and gulped at his coffee. He looked around the office, the messy futon, the old television set, the clothes tossed everywhere.

"You sure you're a real private detective?"

"As far as the state's concerned, yes."

"That isn't doing you any favors. I can't have some amateur playing detective in on this. Someone took something very important to me."

"Excuse the clutter of my office, but I'm no amateur or beginner. I'm very familiar with missing items cases. You should have seen what I had to do during the summer in the zoo. Trust me those guys owe me a favor, big time."

"I don't think you understand. This isn't my grandfather's watch or my mother's necklace. I'm talking about something much more important to all of mankind."

Rolfe straightened his posture and took another sip.

"Alright, well are you going to go around in circles or tell me what it is?"

"I had a gem that I kept on me at all times and now-"

"Now you misplaced it?"

"No, three men broke into my office this morning and robbed me of it."

Rolfe immediately jotted down onto his pad.

"What did these men look like? Do you think you'd be able to point them out if you saw them again?"

"No. They were all wearing Halloween masks with sunglasses and brown hooded sweatshirts. I don't know their skin, hair, or eye color."

"How did you know they were men?"

"Because they were big, loud, and smelled."

"That doesn't rule out anything. I've been with plenty of women who needed a shower or two."

The detective gave a toothy grin, but the TV host didn't smile. Rolfe scribbled more down onto his notes and drank his coffee slowly.

"So this jewel. What's it look like?"

"It's not a jewel, it's a gem."

"I already started your bill if you want to waste the first hour arguing the difference then I'm all for it."

"Gems are worth more, that's all you need to know. You ever hear of garnets?"

"Yeah, I spend most of my time researching gems for fun."

"Oh great so you know about the blue ones?"

"Man, I don't know shit about rocks."

"All you need to know is that it's blue and dangerous."

"What other details can you give me? Is it big? How many sides does it have?"

"It's a dodecahedron and it's probably the size of a good fist."

Rolfe scribbled 'do-deck-a-dron' down with a fat question mark next to it.

"What else can you tell me? What's so important about this jewel? Does it unlock a secret passage to a pirate ship full of gold?"

"If you're not going to take this seriously then I can leave."

"Yeah, I know I'm keeping you from getting back to shouting in the streets. Fine, I'll take it seriously, but you need to tell me what's going on."

Halloween Jack scratched at his head and grabbed the notepad from Rolfe. He scribbled down a drawing of the gem and a large circle. Rolfe glanced at the drawing.

"Alright there's the jewel, but what's the other thing?"

"That's the moon. The full moon to be exact."

"Now the moon's getting involved in this? Did the moon steal it? Were the thieves aliens?"

"I thought you said you'd take this seriously."

"My apologies. Please go on."

Rolfe took the pad back and doodled the moon into a Jack o'lantern.

"Tonight the men who took the gem will use it to summon something that doesn't belong here."

"What's so special about tonight? It's only October 30th. Halloween is tomorrow."

"Yes I know what day it is tomorrow, but you do realize that Halloween starts at midnight, don't you?"

"I always thought spells were done on Halloween night."

"Late tomorrow night would be November 1st. You really don't understand?"

"I have a feeling this is going to be one of these cases where I do a lot of not understanding."

"Get used to it. It comes with the territory. You still in or what?"

"Now you want my help?"

"I didn't say that, but I'll take it. I understand if you don't believe me."

"I believe that you believe and if you're willing to pay for services then it's all the same to me."

Jack rose from his chair and extended his hand. Rolfe stood, shook it, and downed the rest of his coffee.

"You have any idea where to start with this?" said Rolfe.

"Sure, you got a car?"

-

The men climbed into Rolfe's '71 green Chevy Vega hatchback and it only took three tries to get it started. The detective followed the guiding hand of the TV host and off they went.

"Why are they trying to summon something anyway?" said Rolfe, "That never seems like a good idea in the books I've read and movies I've seen. When has it ever gone right?"

"They think it will usher in a new era on Earth. One where they get to rule for once."

"How do you know so much about what their plan is if you don't know who they are?"

"It's the same old bullshit with all of these weirdos. But there is something else that's tipping me off the more I think about it. A strange man came to the studio a few weeks ago asking about the gem. I told him to get lost, but he spouted off his ideology while the guards dragged him away."

"See now that would have been good to know right in the office."

"You think I'm going to tell some detective everything upfront?"

"Only if you want my full cooperation. Where are we headed anyway?"

"To where I think they might be. Keep going in this direction."

They were only driving for twenty minutes, but were already nearing the edge of town where the pavement ended and the trees began. They passed the Black Country Rock diner and soon they were surrounded on both sides of the road with forest. Jack rolled down the window and tossed his arm out, letting it ride the air as they drove. He turned to the detective whose eyes were focused on the winding roads. Rolfe could always feel eyes on him and he darted his own at the TV host.

"What do you have planned for tomorrow's show?" said Rolfe.

Jack withdrew his arm from the window and put his hand in his lap.

"I'm not really concerned with that right now. There's a few more important things bothering me like getting this gem back."

"We'll get it back, don't worry about that. I just want to know what movies I'll be watching on Halloween."

"Fine, I'll spoil it for you. The studio wants me to play Invasion of the Body Snatchers since there's that new version coming out in December. Expect lots of plugs for pod people in the coming months."

"Is that all? You usually play at least three movies."

"Calm down, we're going to show Night of the Living Dead and Karloff's Frankenstein too."

Rolfe tapped his steering wheel with his fingers as though they were piano keys.

"I was hoping to spend the night watching Christopher Lee kill some young women, but alright."

"Teenagers don't care about Dracula anymore. Did you see that last one Hammer made? Van Helsing in China? It was horrible," said Jack.

"I liked that one! It didn't have Lee, but it's always nice to see Cushing."

"You probably like all of them."

Jack stuck his nose out the window and sniffed the air. He waved at the detective to pull off to the side of the road. Rolfe did so and they climbed out of the Vega. There was a small clearing in the trees where they stood.

"Please tell me you have some idea of what you're doing," said Rolfe.

"The weirdo who came into the station mentioned woods and a clearing where the moon would shine down."

"So fucking what? That could be anywhere around here."

Halloween Jack pointed to the gap in the trees.

"Don't you see it? Come on, now it's your turn to follow me."

Jack took off into the woods. Rolfe checked that he had his .38 special and went after the host. It didn't take long for the detective to know what Jack meant. There was a squat concrete building about fifty feet into the forest. On the door in yellow paint was a symbol. It was a wheel with six spokes evenly spaced stemming from the center.

"Not exactly trying to blend in I see. Any idea what it means?" said Rolfe.

"That's the symbol of Rod. He was an ancient Slavic deity. He was their Zeus, Yaweh, Jupiter. One of those higher up gods that no one remembers anymore."

"Seems like someone remembers him if people here in Brixton are worshiping him."

"You may have a point, but what's strange is usually Rod's people were peaceful. They didn't carve people up as offerings, instead they gave bread, cheese, and honey. Those guys who took gem were anything, but civil."

"How do you know all that from what looks like a nuclear symbol?"

Jack let out a laugh.

"A guy can be interested in more than just old horror movies, can't he?"

"I suppose so. What's the plan here?"

"You're asking me? You're the dick here, you tell me."

Rolfe surveyed the building and Jack watched the detective in action. Two small windows were on each wall although they were covered from the inside preventing him from looking in. There were no lights on from what he could although there were also no wires running into the building. He knelt down to the ground and saw tire tracks, but no sign of any vehicle there at the moment.

"What did you find Columbo?" said Jack.

"Looks like they've been driving back here regularly and I don't see a car so I'm assuming no one's in there. You up for going in and taking a peek for ourselves?"

Jack's eyes lit up and Rolfe took that as a yes. They opened the door, stepped inside and saw the blue gem glowing on a table in a corner. Unfortunately a man was sitting at the table rolling it back and forth. His back was towards the two men and they could only see a brown hood drawn up.

"What took you guys so long? I'm fucking starving over here," said the man.

Jack recognized the voice as the witch-man's. He looked at Rolfe and nodded as though the glowing blue gem wasn't enough of a confirmation that they were in the right place. The detective took out his gun and held it at the thief's back. The two men only took two steps before the witch-man turned his body.

"I hope you remembered to get me some extra fries and-"

He was still wearing the witch mask and sunglasses, but both Rolfe and Jack could feel the fear in his eyes behind the lenses. Rolfe kept his gun steady.

"Come on, hand it over," said Jack.

The witch-man tossed the blue gem back into Jack's hands who pocketed it quickly into his jacket.

"How the fuck did you find us?" said the witch-man.

Jack sniffed the air.

"Whatever deodorant you're wearing isn't doing the job," said Jack.

"I'm not wearing any."

"That's the problem," said Rolfe looking around the building.

There was the witch-man in a chair at the table, but the rest of the place was bare bones. A crappy TV, worse than the detective's sat in the corner along with some newspapers, trashed fast food wrappers, and cans of beer. A few sleeping bags were laid out on the floor among the debris. There was also a pistol on the table. *How did I miss that on the first glance over?*

"Don't even think about it," said Rolfe, "Grab that before he does something stupid, will you?"

Jack grabbed the gun and handed it to the detective who holstered it in his suit jacket.

"What should we do with him?" said Rolfe, "I don't exactly see any rope to tie him up with."

"Shouldn't we bring him into the police?" said Jack.

"That's your call to make, not mine. You want to press charges then yes, we'll take him with us."

"What do you think? Do you want to go to jail or do you want to never bother me ever again?" said Jack.

"You're going to let him decide? That's a bad move," said Rolfe.

The witch-man looked at the gun aimed at his chest then at the TV host who was smiling at him next to the short detective.

"You said it was my call to make. Now that depends on what this idiot says," said Jack.

"You serious? You'll leave here and not involve the police?" said the witch-man.

"The less the police know the better when it comes to this stuff. I'm sure we all have real lives we need to get back to."

"That's an easy choice then. You'll never see me or my friends ever again if you let me go," said the witch-man.

"Alright then, come on let's get out of here," said Jack.

"Hold on a second," said Rolfe.

The detective stared at the witch-man before smacking him in the face with his short barrel. The thief winced and Rolfe smacked him once more sending out of his chair to the floor.

"What was that for?" said Jack.

"You got to let him know we mean business," said Rolfe, "Now we can go."

Rolfe and Jack walked out of the front door.

"We have about thirty seconds until he comes after us with another gun," said Rolfe.

The detective sprinted down the path and Jack followed quickly this time without prompting.

His green Vega was where he left it. They climbed in and he turned the key. The engine revved, but it wouldn't start. Jack slammed his hands down on the dashboard.

Rolfe turned the key again and the response was the same. He found his body being jerked down by Jack.

"Stay down, I see someone coming," said Jack.

The detective peeked up to see a jeep turning down into the path that they had come from. Jack saw the taillights go into the woods and he popped back up.

"Are you fucking kidding me? You can't get this piece of junk started? What are we going to do?"

Rolfe ignored the TV host who was screaming in his car. *I should have ignored him when he was screaming in the streets. Now I'm going to be lucky if I get out of this alive. Come on old girl, start up for your favorite dick.*

He turned it once more and still nothing.

"Fuck it, let's foot it," said Jack.

The TV host jumped out of the car and headed down the road before Rolfe could say a word. Rolfe took off after him. The two ran down the side of the road and it wasn't long before they heard the engine of a Jeep on their asses.

"You sons of bitches! Get back here with that jewel!"

It was the skull-man driving the jeep with the pumpkin-man and witch-man hanging out the door-less sides. They were swinging baseball bats in the air. Practicing their technique for what they'd do to the running men if they were caught.

"See? I'm not the only who thinks it is a jewel," said Rolfe.

"Yeah, you're in real good company," said Jack.

The Jeep whirred past them, Jack ducked the swing, but Rolfe wasn't so lucky. He felt himself going down once more beyond his control. He hit the ground and his eyes were closing as he saw the masked men attacking Jack.

-

Rolfe awoke to find himself blindfolded and bound. *I guess those bastards had some tape or rope after all.*

He squirmed and wiggled his body, trying to feel if anything was loose. There wasn't and he heard a voice in response to his movements.

"How about you quit flailing so much or I'll make you stop," said the skull-man.

"How about you take off this blindfold and let me know what the hell is going on," said Rolfe.

"What else do you need to know? We beat and tied you up," said the witch-man.

"Just take the damn blindfold off, will you?" said the pumpkin-man.

The cloth was removed from the detective's eyes and he found himself outside in the woods. It was way past sundown and the stars were twinkling, but there was no sign of the moon. *I thought these spells happened under a full moon. Isn't that what Jack drew in my notes? Wait a minute, where is Jack?*

Rolfe turned his head to see a still passed out Jack also with duct taped hands to a chair which he himself realized he was tied to.

A fire was going at a steady rate with the three masked thieves sitting around it. Rolfe and Jack were about fifteen feet away from the men. They were even still wearing their sunglasses despite the dark night. The skull-man had the blue gem in his hand, tossing it up and down like a game of lonesome catch. The witch-man had the detective's revolver, opening and closing it over and over to hear the clicking sound it made. The pumpkin-man was reading a book with the same six spoke wheel symbol on the cover that Rolfe had seen earlier.

"Excuse me, but how long was I out for?" said Rolfe.

The skull-man turned and looked at the others.

"Couple of hours," he said.

"That's all you'll tell me? Fine. What time is it now?"

"A few minutes to midnight," said the witch-man.

"A few minutes until the world changes," said the pumpkin-man.

"If you don't mind me asking, what exactly are you three planning to do?" said Rolfe.

"You'll see, you only have a few more minutes to wait. Don't get antsy now," said the skull-man.

"Yeah, in-fact let's get your friend up too cause we need to ask him something real important," said the witch-man.

The three men went over to Jack and tore off his blindfold. They smacked his face with their hands until Jack stirred awake. He grumbled out of unconsciousness and his torso jolted at being brought back.

"Halloween Jack! It's so good to see you again," said the skull-man.

"We didn't think you'd want to hang out after what happened this morning," said the pumpkin-man.

"I'm telling you two, he can't get enough of us. He wanted to make sure his kind donation was put to good use, isn't that right, Jack?" said the witch-man.

"Donation my ass. You stole that from me. Twice now," said Jack.

"Come on now, Jack, we're only trying to lighten the mood. Have some fun, won't you? We're about to have a lot of fun ourselves."

Rolfe's fingers dug into the tape around him. He slowly, but surely was ripping them apart. *It's a good thing I didn't clip my nails last night after Bao made fun of me for them being longer than hers.*

"Weren't we going to ask him something?" said the skull-man.

"Ah, yeah, that's right. We were," said the pumpkin-man, "I think you should do the honors considering your fine history with our guest here."

The pumpkin-man gestured to the witch-man and Rolfe could see the grin on the witch's face by the way the mask twitched.

"Well Halloween Jack. What's the best way to put this? I suppose there's no good way other than bluntly. We need a human sacrifice tonight. Now we were going to draw straws between the three of us, but now we have something even better. We have two potential sacrifices right here in front of us. After all, you two dropped in on us and how could refuse such an opportunity?"

"You can't be serious," said Jack.

"Of course we're serious. You think we went through all this trouble for some mischief night prank?" said the pumpkin-man.

The three masked men chuckled loudly and the gem's glow increased.

"You must understand, we're not monsters and we wish no one had to die, but unfortunately someone does need to. The good news is that we only need one sacrifice. So we're giving you a choice just like your buddy there gave you earlier. Who do you think we should offer up? You or your friend?" said the witch-man.

Rolfe looked at Jack and nodded. Jack shook his head at him.

"I'll do it," said Rolfe.

The men chuckled again.

"No, no, it's up to Jack to decide," said the witch-man, "What do you say, Halloween Jack?"

"Fine, kill me, but only if you let him go," said Jack.

"Of course we'll let him go. Right after he watches you die," said the skull-man.

The pumpkin-man whipped out a knife and cut Jack free from the chair. Rolfe was still using his own claws to pick apart the duct tape that kept him bound. *Work faster you stupid hands. What do I keep you for if you're going to be slow when I need you most?*

The masked men took Jack over to the fire by gun point. The witch-man checked his watch and it read midnight.

"Right on time, too. Happy Halloween, Halloween Jack," said the witch-man.

The skull-man dropped the blue gem by Jack's feet and it was softly glowing. The pumpkin-man grabbed the book and the three men read from it.

"On this new moon on this All Hallow's Eve, let all good things be born," they chanted.

Rolfe's fingers scrapped faster. He could feel his bonds loosening. He pulled and his onc hand was free.

"Let all good things be born! Let all good things be born!" they chanted.

They repeated the chant over and over. Jack stood in silence watching the blue gem glow stronger. A light began to pour out above the gem and all the men could feel a sudden wind pick up. The leaves under the trees flew into the air in a small whirl wind. They were being sucked into themselves as the gem glowed brighter and the blue light grew taller.

"Let's all good things be born," they continued.

Rolfe had both hands free now and he was trying his hardest to remove the tape from his legs.

The masked men turned to each other as though to smile that their spell was working. The blue light was now spinning within the gale it had created. It stood higher than all the men and a force was pulling Jack into it.

"Help me, Rolfe. Please, help me."

His voice was crackling. It reminded Rolfe of when he'd talk into the fan as a kid during a hot summer day. Rolfe ripped off the rest of the tape as the men continued their chant. The detective ran towards Jack, but there was little he could do. Jack's legs were already sucked into the void and he was phasing in and out of view. Rolfe grabbed for Jack's hand and his own hand went right through it. Jack shook his head and then he was gone.

The blue void still spun and ground below was shaking. Something was coming through the other side. It jutted out quickly and Rolfe fell to his ass trying to avoid it. He crawled backwards to hide behind a tree. The three men stopped their chanting and started applauding. The detective's vision cleared and he saw a set of hairy arms coming through the light. A second later the whole being was standing where Jack was. It was seven feet of hair, claws, and eyes. Yes it had glowing yellow eyes on its furry face with short pointed ears, but it also had a large eye on each shoulder that stared at the men. Saliva dripped from its jaws and it let out a howl of anger. Rolfe held his distance from behind the tree. *Looks like something I'd see on 'In Search Of.'*

"We did it, we actually did it," said the skull-man.

"The drekavec is ours!" said the pumpkin-man.

"Give thanks to those who brought you here," said the witch-man.

The creature turned to the three men and growled. It charged them with claws extended and slashed at the pumpkin-man. His throat exploded in a geyser of blood and he fell face forward to the ground. The skull-man screamed, grabbed his gun and shot at the drekavec. The bullet hit the giant eye on its left shoulder. A mixture of pus and blood squirted onto the skull-man and he was torn in half at the torso before he could wipe his eyes clean.

The witch-man emptied Rolfe's revolver into the creature's chest. The drekavec, slow and steady, stomped at the last man standing and grabbed his arm that was still clicking the hammer of the empty gun. The beast ripped off the witch-man's arm and shoved it through the man's chest. The witch-man fell and so did the drekavec. Rolfe had watched it all from afar and went over to the creature. It was laid down on its back, breathing heavily, and gurgling blood out its mouth. Its eyes were squinted and Rolfe saw a universal language in them, one that was crying out in fear. The detective knelt down and grabbed its fur covered hand until the light and pain went away.

-

What do you do when there's a mess to clean up and don't want to answer any questions? You cash in favors. That's what Edgar Rolfe did. He called the local mafia, the Corbuccis and they didn't ask a goddamn thing when burying a monster and three men. It was all over before the sun even came up. Rolfe spent most of the day sleeping. It was only when he heard a knock at the door that he decided to wake up. A little ghost and his mother were the first trick or treaters of the night. Rolfe tossed him a candy bar and didn't even check out the mom before closing the door and slumping in his chair. He turned on the TV, but there was no movie marathon to be had. He switched to the news as the once blue gem now sat colorless on his desk.

Solstice Special

Decembers in Brixton, New Jersey are cold, bitter, and loud. Not only are people noisy, but they're flashy as well. Garish decorations fill the windows of houses and storefronts. One of those large Christmas trees even gets thrown up in the middle of town. For a few weeks the whole town turns into a winter wonderland.

It all wouldn't be that bad if it weren't for the fact that Brixton tradition calls for early decorating. The people made a conscious decision back in '63 to decorate the day after Thanksgiving. While others shopped on Black Friday, Brixton put up lights, tinsel, and those wooden candy canes. But maybe they do it because the days are short, freezing, and a reminder that life is fleeting. Or maybe it was so the town could look joyful yet somber with its flashy décor against the gray skies.

One of Brixton's youngest residents was both merry in appearance and mind as he played in his front yard. His name was Howie Lane, he was five years old, and he lived with his sister and father in a small house that wasn't too far from the big tree on main street. Sure it was cold outside, but there was little else to do for a kid his age on a Saturday morning. He sat in the dirt with his winter coat tight and toys to keep him company. The war against the rocks and sticks was real enough to the five year old in the mud and his 'men' that stood by him. He had himself a nice platoon to command around him; a red dump truck acting as a tank, a monstrous yellow tyrannosaurus as the infantry, and his favorite, a stuffed zebra that was his second in command. The zebra wasn't spared any bloodshed or rather dirt-shed as it was covered in filth and grime from many days of play.

But the rocks and sticks weren't the only enemy out there to harm Howie's soldiers. The boy played in his head and didn't notice the figure coming from down the road. They were taller than him as nearly everyone is when you're five and they moved faster too. Two long legs made a stride look easy to the kid. The figure's face was completely covered as was the rest of their body. They ran into the Lane's yard, straight up to the boy, and ripped the zebra from his hands. The child tried to fight back, but the whole ordeal was over in less than a minute. The masked thief had stripped him of his favorite toy and most loyal soldier then took off. Howie Lane was left alone once more. He wiped the tears from his eyes and headed inside.

—

Private eye, Edgar Rolfe was sitting at the counter of his favorite restaurant which happened to sit under his office. He was slurping down some lo mein while the cook, Sun Wu grabbed the dick another beer. The server, Bao Wu, was resting on a stool after cleaning up after a customer. She was heavily pregnant to the point where she might pop if someone bumped her too hard. Rolfe sipped at his beer between bites and admiring his surroundings. The Chinese restaurant hadn't escaped being decorated with Christmas cheer. Wreaths and garlands were in view no matter where one's eyes rested. They even had an aluminum tree in the corner with red balls hanging off it.

He turned his head back to his plate and the graveyard of beer bottles that were started to pile up early on a Saturday. He was on his fifth and his good friend, Sun Wu kept bringing him more on the house. Who was he to refuse such a generous offer? Especially when he didn't care that his rent was late again, but still he was a detective at his core. Curiosity got the best of him and he wanted to know what the catch was.

"It's not that I'm not being grateful, but I have to know. What's the deal with you feeding me all this free booze, man?" said Rolfe.

"Don't you 'man' me," said Sun, "What's the matter? I can't give my friend a few drinks during the holidays?"

Bao Wu's clutched her large belly as she let out a laugh.

"That's what you're going with?" she said, "You can do better than that."

The cook smiled and got busy preparing an order that came in over the phone. Rolfe looked to Bao for a real answer.

"Alright, spill it. What's going on here?" said Rolfe.

"As you can clearly see I'm pregnant," said Bao.

"As anyone can see, no offense."

She chuckled again and her stomach lifted with it.

"Yes, well, Sun got tired of me complaining every time he had a beer so he decided to quit drinking until we can both share a glass of wine together. Unfortunately he had built up an extra stock of beer before agreeing to stop."

"I see. That means I get to drink it all?"

Sun directed his attention back to the detective and his wife.

"Hey, it can be both things, can't it? I can be a good friend and also a good husband. Two birds, one stone as they say."

The detective shoveled more food and beer into his stomach and wiped at his mouth with the sleeve of his black suit. He noticed some stains were growing in numbers on his clothes. Luckily his brown dress shirt was perfect for blending with with the drops of lo mein that had fallen onto it. He took another swig and lifted the beer in a motion of solidarity with the couple.

"Suppose there's nothing wrong with that," said Rolfe.

The cook let out a bigger smile while managing a pan full of noodles.

"Great, I'm glad you think so."

He paused on his cooking, went to their large fridge, pulled out two six packs and placed them on the counter in front of the detective.

"Go ahead, drink up," said Sun.

"I know I'm on my holiday break, but I don't think I should be drinking this much in one day."

"Who said you have to drink it all in one day? I don't care when or if you drink, I don't want it here anymore. The temptation to pop one open grows stronger every minute being around her."

Bao perked up. She waddled over to the detective at the counter and leaned over to see her husband. He was crouched down in hiding under the guise of grabbing a bag of rice.

"You say that like I haven't been a pleasure," she said.

He peeked up and headed over to a boiling pot.

"Oh yes, your random cravings at three in the morning have not disrupted my sleep at all."

"Think of it as a little preview for what's to come when the baby gets here."

"Hopefully we have a few more weeks until then. I'd like to get at least one night's rest before years of broken sleep."

"You me and both, but I don't think we'll be that lucky. The doctor said the baby could decide to come any day now."

"Please don't speak such ideas out loud," said Sun.

Rolfe finished his plate of food, gulped down the rest of his current beer, and dusted himself off.

"I think I better get back upstairs," he said.

"Already? You don't want to stay down here with a bickering couple?" said Bao.

"I'm sure he has better things to do like start his decorating or watch one of those Christmas specials he loves," said Sun.

"Or maybe I need to sleep off this buzz you've been feeding me all morning," said Rolfe.

He grabbed the two six packs of beer and headed for the door. He turned back to see the couple embracing in a hug and sharing a kiss. The detective nodded at them.

"Don't worry, I'll be back for more food later," he said.

"Oh we're never worried about that," said Bao.

"I even bought some extra ingredients for your potsickers You're going to love them."

"Sometimes I think you don't ever want to get rid of me," said Rolfe.

Edgar Rolfe felt the cold air greet him for a moment while he climbed up the stairs to his office. He closed the door behind him, put most of the beers in in a mini-fridge and sat down on the futon that was his bed. He lived where he worked and his work was his life. Most of the time anyway. Now it was time to drink another beer and see what was on TV. He'd be damned if he was going to decorate his office. There was hardly a mention of the holiday within the walls of Edgar Rolfe. He didn't hate the holidays, but the rest of Brixton did enough to celebrate without it having to invade his personal space.

He sipped from the bottle while he flipped through the channels until he landed on a nice looking woman dressed as Mrs. Claus singing with a band behind her. *A nice two weeks of doing nothing, but relaxing, drinking, and getting fatter. I can't think of a better way to pass the time. I hope this woman makes it a habit to keep singing too.* He took off his suit jacket, kicked off his shoes, and let himself enjoy the all familiar Christmas tunes. His eyes were nearly closed, ready for a nap when he heard a knock at his door.

His eyes popped back open and he stood up with a bounce. He didn't even spill his beer as he did so. The door opened and he had to look down to see who was there. The figure was a lot smaller than those who normally knocked. It was little Howie Lane standing and fighting back tears that were already in his eyes. Rolfe placed his beer down on a shelf and cleared his throat.

"Can I help you with something? Are you alright? Are you lost?" said Rolfe.

The boy wiped his eyes and nodded.

"When my dad drives by here he always points and says, 'This is the detective's house.' Is that true?"

"It's true. Why does a kid like you need a detective? Is your dad okay? Did something happen to him?"

Howie Lane nodded again.

"He's okay, but I need your help."

"Kid, I don't know what I can do for you."

"My name is Howie, not 'kid.'"

A light went off in the detective's head.

"Ah, you're Brian Lane's son. I thought I've seen you around before. Well, Howie, I think you better get back home before your dad gets worried. Does he know you're here?"

The kid shook his head no.

"But I'm not going anywhere until you help me."

Rolfe could see the tears starting up again in the kid's eyes. The air was frigid and he sighed.

"Fine, come in and get warm, and tell me what's wrong, but then I'm bringing you home."

Howie stepped inside and Rolfe shut the door. He led the kid to the chair in front of his desk and he hopped onto it.

Howie looked around the office, seeing the small TV, the messy futon, and lack of decorations while he waited for Rolfe to rejoin him. The detective slipped his jacket and shoes back on before bringing a mug of hot chocolate over.

"You like hot cocoa?" said Rolfe.

"Sure," said Howie.

Rolfe took his place behind his desk, beer in hand, and drank.

"My winter vacation just started kid so this better be good. Now what's so important that you'd come to a stranger for help?"

Howie drank from his mug of hot chocolate as if he were downing a shot of whiskey.

"It's my toy zebra. He's missing."

Rofle let out a laugh. It was not only because he found it humorous, but it was also a relief. *For a second I was worried I'd have to take a case on my break. I thought this little kid saw his old man get gutted.*

The detective let himself relax once more and even took a generous swig from his beer.

"You're here because you lost a toy?"

"No. I didn't lose him! He was taken from me."

"I'll bite. Taken how?"

"Taken! Someone came up to me and stole it."

"Who would want to steal a toy from a kid?"

Rolfe put down the beer and examined the child's eyes. They were once again on the verge of waterworks. *God damn this kid cries a lot in front of strangers. I always left that in the bedroom. I guess I could at least entertain the idea.*

"Alright you say someone stole your zebra. What can you tell me about them? What did they look like?"

"They were big."

"Everyone's big to you. Did you see their face?"

"No, they had no face."

"You mean it was covered?"

Howie nodded.

"Did you see anything that you could identify them with?"

The kid's face shifted into puzzlement. There was a moment of silence and Rolfe watched the child while he waited for a response. There was none.

"I understand you've probably never been asked these types of questions before. I'll try to make it easier on you. Did you see their eyes? Their skin? Their hair? Was it a man or a woman? Anything?"

Howie shook his head at all of the detective's questions. He took a giant gulp of the hot cocoa and put the mug on Rolfe's desk.

"You mean to tell me that someone came up to you in a disguise, grabbed your zebra, and ran off? Maybe we're dealing with the boogeyman here."

"Do you think you can find him?"

"The zebra or the boogeyman? Either way it's not looking good. I don't know where I'd start. I don't exactly do missing toy cases. You understand that, don't you kid?"

Howie nodded, sipped from his mug, hopped off the chair and headed for the door without prompting.

"I'm sorry for wasting your time," he said.

Rolfe jumped to his feet off his chair and away from his desk.

"Hold on kid, you really think I was going to let you walk home alone? How do you think it would sit with me if I did that?"

Howie turned back, paused, and stared at Rolfe. The detective opened a wardrobe, pulled out a thick long gray jacket and put it on. He nodded at the kid and out the door they went.

—

The air had managed to become colder since the last time Rolfe was outside. He had decided to walk the kid home instead of driving him. There were a few reasons for this. One, he knew where the kid lived and it wasn't too far. Two, he knew that there was a store nearby where he could pick something up for the Wu baby to be. But most importantly was three, and that was he was tipsy and needed to walk off the buzz he was carrying around with him. His steps were already seeming heavy and there wasn't any snow to blame it on. Six beers might not bother a taller man, but Rolfe was on the shorter side of five-eight.

Rolfe was trying to speed the process along and he found himself having to pause every few feet waiting for the kid to catch up. Howie was too distracted by all the decorations. He was taking his time to look at the same trees, lights, and wreaths that were put up year after year. *I suppose they are still new to him. It might be the first time he's ever seen these old things for longer than a split second. Hell, everything's new to him at his age. Take it in kid, it only goes down from here.*

They stood outside a squat two story house that was painted blue. It had four windows from the front and a wreath hung in each one. A family of white wooden reindeer were grazing on the lawn. There were four in total; two smaller ones and two bigger ones with one of those having the expected antlers. Howie seemed particularly fixated on one of the smaller reindeer nuzzling its mother. His little feet carried him closer with his arm stretched out towards the lawn ornament.

Rolfe was about to tap the kid on the shoulder when they heard a voice from the door of the house.

"Hey there."

The two looked to see an old man standing there. His voice had a kindness to it. It was loud enough for them to hear, but not fear the greeting. He was dressed in a dark green jacket with a matching ski cap. His whiskers matched his age, long, white, and fully cheeked. He joined the two who were standing on her lawn admiring his set up. Rolfe looked towards the man with a squint in his eyes. *Oh great, here comes one of the locals. Good job loitering until he noticed us, kid.*

"Hey yourself. Hope we're not bothering you. The kid wanted a closer look is all," said Rolfe.

"No bother at all. You're that private detective. Rolfe, isn't it?"

He was taller and older than the private eye and usually a statement like that would be an invitation for either an argument or wanting something for free. However the dick detected neither from the intonation given from the man.

"Yeah that's me."

"And he's Howie Lane."

"Right again. I'm sorry, I don't recall your name or meeting you before."

"That's because you haven't met me before. I know you from seeing you walking up your stairs with the sign hanging above. The child I know from his father."

"That does explain things I suppose."

"I forgot my manners. My name is Jol."

The old man extended his hand and Rolfe shook it. They were clearly working hands from the grip, but with enough grace as to not hurt the dick. The two men locked eyes and Rolfe could easily tell one of the old man's was glass.

"That's not a very common name around here."

"That's because it's not from around here. It's Icelandic."

"Iceland, huh? Can't say that I've ever been or know much about it, but it's nice to meet you."

"Likewise Mr. Rolfe."

"If you don't mind though we were on our way to getting Howie here home."

"Not at all. I have to get ready for work myself. I hope you both have a nice day."

The boy nodded at the old man who returned the gesture. He walked over to Rolfe and they continued on their way to Howie's house.

The kid wasn't as distracted by the other decorations between the old man's place and his own. He kept pace with the detective and they made it back to his home within ten minutes. Howie started to run up the short stairs to his front door as soon as they hit his driveway. Rolfe followed in pursuit and nearly walked in after him, but paused and was about to knock when Mr. Lane appeared at the entrance. Howie hung by his father's leg without grasping it.

"Where the hell have you been?" said Lane.

"I told you someone took my zebra. I went to get help," said Howie gesturing to the detective in the doorway.

"You went and bothered this man? He doesn't have time for your games, Howie."

"I'm sorry, it's just-"

"It's just nothing. I was worried sick about you. I went up and down the street looking for you. And here you were wasting this man's time when he has real crimes to solve."

Rolfe saw the tears start to form in the kid's eyes again. It was starting to become an annoying habit to witness.

"I'm sorry-"

"Don't apologize to me. Apologize to Mr. Rolfe here," said Lane.

Howie turned to the detective with a frown.

"I'm sorry, Mr. Rolfe."

"That's good enough for now. Go on and get to your room, I'll talk to you after I deal with our guest here."

Howie marched up the stairs trying to make his foot steps as loud as he could with his tiny stomps.

Mr. Lane invited Rolfe in and he offered the detective a chair at the kitchen table which he declined. The kitchen and table itself were placed right by the front door. Mr. Lane grabbed a beer and offered that too to the detective which he also declined. So Mr. Lane settled in with a beer and Rolfe stood more towards the door.

"I want to apologize for my son. I know you have better things to do with your time."

"Don't worry, Mr. Lane, he wasn't a problem. I didn't come here because I'm mad. I only wanted to make sure he got home safe. Don't be too hard on him for my sake. He didn't disturb my day."

"That's a relief to hear, Mr. Rolfe, but don't tell Howie that. We can't have him thinking he can take off whenever he wants without saying something."

"Is this something he does often? Run away I mean," said Rolfe.

Lane wiped at his brow before drinking from his beer.

"No. This is the only time he's ever done anything like this," said Lane.

"He seemed really upset, Mr. Lane. I was worried something was wrong."

"That's because he's a cry baby. So he lost a toy. What can we do about it?"

It was a different voice. A very soft high voice coming from the other room. The source made herself known a second later when she walked in from the living room. It was a young woman, around 15 or 16 according to the detective's eyes. She had a spindly build and dressed in a blue and white stripped nursing uniform. *She must be one of those blue teen volunteers at the hospital.* She glanced at the detective, grabbed a bottle of pop from the fridge, and took a seat next to her father.

"I didn't even notice you had slipped in. This is my daughter, Jodie." said Lane.

"Yeah I got done early today. They said it'll be my last short day until after New Years," she took a slow sip of her soda and glanced at the detective again, "It's nice to meet you Mr. Rolfe. Dad, here, always says nice things about you when we drive by your office."

Rolfe nodded at the man sitting across from him.

"I appreciate that. And now I don't mean to take up any more of your time."

"We understand. We know a detective like you needs to get back to work," said Lane.

"Are you sure you can't stay Mr. Rolfe? We have plenty of beer and cookies. I could even make you dinner for helping bring my brother back safe and sound."

Rolfe look at Mr. Lane who didn't seem opposed to the idea. That only made it worse for the detective to turn the offer down.

"Thanks, but I do need to get going. Maybe some other time."

He headed for the door and stopped when he heard the sounds of tiny footsteps rushing down the stairs. A photo was clutched in Howie's hands and he held it out for Rolfe to take. The picture was of an older woman sitting with the boy in her lap and the little zebra in his. They were in a park on a warm summer's day judging by their lack of long sleeves or coats. Smiles were on all their faces, even the stuffed toy had a glint in its eye. *One of those few perfect moments that get captured on film.*

"That's what he looks like," said Howie.

"Good to know. I'll send him this way if I find him," said Rolfe, "May I suggest something to you? You should try looking around your room. He may turn up. I lost plenty of toys only to find them later."

He handed the photo back to the kid, gave a wave to the those at the table and headed out the door. He started down the driveway when something caught his attention in the dirt. It was on the front lawn, not too far from the road. Rolfe knelt down to get a closer look. It was a long black and white strip of cloth with a black tuft on the end. *The zebra's tail? Could the kid be telling the truth?*

He paused and nearly turned back towards the house. Instead he pocketed the evidence and continued on.

—

The beer buzz was nearing its end when Rolfe reached one of Brixton's finest department stores, Big Blue Shop. The name never made sense to the detective since they carried all colors. He went in and there was the expected crowd shopping during December. It too didn't escape the decorations that swept over the town. Not only did they sell them, but corner caps and ceilings had hanging snowflakes, balls, and gingerbread men everywhere.

He made his way down the aisles looking for something to get the forthcoming baby. *What the hell do you get a baby anyway? What does a baby want?* Rolfe found himself staring at socks, stuffed bears, and pacifiers. *We don't even know if it's a boy or a girl yet.*

The detective was about to give up when he found something that clicked right with him. It was a small yellow blanket with red satin trim going around it. On the blanket itself were three elephants. They were in a row with the middle one being smaller than those on its sides. *A little elephant family.* He snatched it as though it would disappear if he didn't.

He got in line and it moved much faster than expected. The others in line weren't nasty, weren't paying in pennies, and seemed to practice basic hygiene. They stood in their winter coats, one by one, approaching the cashier then disappearing in a smooth fashion. It was the detective's turn now. The cashier was a teenage boy who asked Rolfe if he needed anything else. The detective looked around the store and then behind the register. That's where he saw it. A brand new stuffed zebra. He pointed it out to the pimple faced kid and gladly bought it along with the blanket.

The chill walk back to his office had sobered him up completely. He tossed the gifts in the trunk of his '71 green Chevy Vega and was nearly about to hit his steps when Sun appeared at the restaurant's door. His face was flush, sweaty, and distressed.

"What's going on?" said Rolfe.

"It's time, it's coming, we need to go now. Are you ready?" said Sun.

"Sure, I'm ready. Where's Bao?"

"She's inside, come on and help me walk her to your car."

The two men went back in and did just that. Bao's teeth were clenched with pain and they helped her waddle to the detective's car. Sun got into the back seat with his wife and Rolfe took the helm behind the wheel.

The Vega burned out of the driveway and onto Brixton's roads headed for the hospital. Bao was panting in the back while Sun tended to her by letting her squeeze his hand into a paste. Rolfe could see the sweat dripping off both their brows in his back seat. *Sometimes I'm more than happy that I was born a man.* He peeled the wheels around a corner and they were met with a problem. Two flashing cop cars were parked in the middle of the road where they were going to turn down. In the far off distance there was something else. They were a speck at first, but soon the band's music grew louder and closer.

It was Brixton High's Christmas parade slowly marching down the street. A bunch of teens dressed in red and green with their instruments blasting proudly in the afternoon. Rolfe could even make out a small float built on a car coming their way.

"This might be a problem," said Rolfe.

"What's going on up there? Why'd we stop?" said Bao.

Sun leaned forward from the backseat through the windshield.

"Maybe they'll let us through. Let me go talk to them," said Sun.

"Hold on there, better it be me," said Rolfe.

The dick jumped out of his car and ran up to one of the cop cars. He got lucky in that he immediately recognized the officer. One Leonard Cake easily identifiable from his badge and young voice that was happily chatting through his window to the other car. Cake of course also easily knew Rolfe from his height, demeanor, and wrinkles around his eyes.

"Leonard, what's happening here?" said Rolfe.

"What do you mean, Rolfe? The kids are having their parade like always," said Leonard.

"Yeah, I can see that, what I don't know is why it's happening so early. I thought it was going to be three hours from now."

"Weather calls for rain tonight."

"That's it? So you're having it early?"

"Calls for rain, Rolfe."

"Okay, fine, but I have a woman in my backseat who's about to pop out a kid and I need to get her to the hospital. Do you think you could pause the kids and let us through?"

Leonard looked to the other officer who shook his head.

"No can do, Rolfe."

"Why not? Hold on, let me guess. Because of the rain?"

"We can't shut down a parade because of a pregnant woman."

"The whole reason they're having a parade is because of a pregnant woman!"

A scream came out from the back of the Vega. Sun popped his head out from the window.

"What's the deal, Rolfe? Can we get through or not?"

Both officers shook their heads.

"Fine, we'll double back and go the long way, but none of you bastards better pull me over for speeding. And do me a favor, call ahead and tell them we're coming," said Rolfe.

Rolfe climbed back into his seat, turned the car around, and sped down the road.

It took fifteen minutes longer to reach the hospital. This year's parade seemed particularly long as many streets were blocked off. Rolfe bobbed and weaved through the alleys until they were a block away from the hospital. Bao held her own while the Vega twisted and turned around corners faster than it should have. The hospital was in view now and Rolfe pulled up to the front.

A couple of nurses were waiting for them at the door with a wheelchair. *At least those cops managed to do something nice for once. Must be a damn Christmas miracle.*

Rolfe and Sun helped Bao into the chair. The nurses sped her away and Sun turned back to the car.

"What are you doing? Go with your wife," said Rolfe.

"I need to get her bag," said Sun.

He looked into the back seat, but nothing was there.

"I can't believe this. I forgot the damn bag. How could I do this? We have nothing for the baby, nothing for Bao."

Rolfe went to his trunk and grabbed the shopping bag with the blanket and zebra toy. He took them both out and handed the blanket to Sun.

"Here, I got this for the baby," said Rolfe, "The zebra's for someone else."

Sun smiled and extended his hand for a brief handshake which Rolfe accepted.

"And don't worry, I'll go back and get the bag for you two. Now get in there. Your wife needs you."

"Thank you," said Sun.

Rolfe walked with Sun until they were both inside then started back for his car. He held the little zebra in his hands and smiled at it. The ringing bell of a Santa cut through the night by the hospital door. It was a nice looking Santa with a full white beard and a nice red suit. Next to him was a donation bin, ready for toys to be given to those kids who needed them most.

Rolfe was about to climb into his car when the Santa called out to him.

"Oh is that for the bin?" said Santa.

The detective turned around with the zebra in hand. The Santa looked familiar. As he should since they met this afternoon. It was the old man Jol in a bright red suit ringing the bell in the cold night. He had his one good eye on the zebra that Rolfe was holding with a grin.

"I didn't think I'd see you again so soon," said Jol, "Are you here to donate? Is that zebra for the bin?"

Rolfe looked down at the stuffed toy.

"Well, actually it's for-"

"We haven't had many good donations this week. Sure there's been some baseballs, footballs, and cheap dolls and the kids will love them all the same, but nothing truly special."

"I wasn't planning on donating it, I'm sorry," said Rolfe.

The smile didn't leave the Santa's face even after that news.

"That's a shame to hear because we've got an old tattered one here. A new one would be much better," sad Jol.

"Really? Do you mind if I see it?"

The Santa bent over, fished the toy out, and the detective nearly gasped. It was Howie's zebra alright. It was even missing its tail.

"This might sound unusual, but would you take a trade?" said Rolfe.

"You want this old beaten up toy?" said Jol.

"I don't, but I know a boy who would. It would make his Christmas."

"How could I say no to that?"

Rolfe handed over the new zebra and the Santa gave the old one in return. For a split second the detective swore he could see the glint in its beady eye that was there in the photo.

"I've got to get this someone, but I'll be back," said Rolfe.

"Merry Christmas Edgar Rolfe."

"Yeah, Merry Christmas."

—

The ride back was much easier than the ride there. The parade had ended and the streets were empty. Not a single one was left blocked. It was as if the whole event didn't occur. Rolfe grabbed the overnight bag from the Wus restaurant and drove to the Lane's house.

Jodie Lane was the one to answer the door. She said her dad wasn't home and for the detective to come inside. He did as he was told and stood by the kitchen table once more while she sat down with another soda.

"So you decided to come back for dinner? My father should be home any minute. I already have the meatloaf cooking in the oven."

"I'm afraid I'm not here for dinner. This will only take a minute. Is Howie here? I came here to return something to him," said Rolfe.

The detective reached into his coat pocket and pulled out the beaten up zebra. He could see the disgust on Jodie's eyes after he placed it on the table.

"Why would you bring that back?" she said.

"Why would you put it in a donation bin?"

"I don't know what you're talking about."

"Yeah, the girl who volunteers at the hospital where I happened to find this toy doesn't know what I'm talking about."

She sat in silence and stared down into the soda bottle.

"You mind calling him down here? I want to make sure he gets it."

The teenage girl hollered for her brother who slowly came down the stairs. His pace picked up when he saw it was Rolfe standing in his kitchen.

Rolfe tossed the zebra to the kid and he hugged it. Tears of joy filled his eyes this time instead of pain. He hugged the detective's leg and danced around the kitchen.

"He's back, he's back, he's really back!" said Howie.

"I nearly forgot," said Rolfe pulling out the torn off tail from his pocket.

"You think you can sew that back on for him?" said Rolfe to the girl.

"I can. Howie why don't you wait upstairs and I'll be up to fix him for you."

The boy smiled and hugged the zebra. He held him tight as he went up the stairs, filling in the toy on recent events. The detective stood in the kitchen like a pillar.

"You should consider yourself lucky your father isn't here. Make sure nothing happens to that zebra or I will come back for dinner, do you understand?"

The girl nodded.

—

The hours waiting in the hospital lobby passed quickly. Rolfe napped, watched the TV, and caught up on the crossword section of every paper that was left out in the room. He was nodding off when Sun approached him from the double doors. His grin stretched ear to ear and his walk had swagger. Rolfe stood to meet him.

"What's the news?"

"He's happy and healthy and so is his mother."

"A little boy? Congratulations my friend."

"We're calling him Ido."

"That's a fine name. A very fine name."

"Would you like to meet him?"

"There's nothing else I'd rather do right now."

"That's good to hear. Do you mind working the Christmas shift in the restaurant as well?"

"What kind of uncle would I be if I didn't help out when you needed me? It's not like I can hide either."

The two men laughed and headed through the double doors to Bao's room.

About

Michael Polillo holds a bachelor's in journalism from Rowan University. He lives in southern New Jersey and grew up on a steady diet of kaiju movies, spaghetti westerns, and pulp books. Now he writes horror, dark comedies, and science fiction.

Subscribe to my mailing list to stay up to date on my latest release http://eepurl.com/gRQ4Qn

Follow me on Twitter @MikePolillo and Instagram @countpupper

Other Titles

I'm Sal: The Soft Boiled Mobster – A crime thriller with mobster Sal Corbucci about his journey to find a missing daughter of a retired boxer.

Armordillo – A giant armadillo is on a rampage in a small Texas town and it's up to journalist Jack Strafer to find a way to stop it.

The Girl with the Electric Eye – A sci-fi western with bounty hunter Ashley Morris searching for the woman who took her eye.

We're Bitches – A horror about three men stuck in a beach house full of lady werewolves looking to make them their next meal.

Black Country Rock – A thriller about two small time thieves who steal from the wrong person.

All titles available in paperback and ebook.